D0093818

# The Doctor
# Dines in Prague

ALSO BY ROBIN HATHAWAY

DOCTOR FENIMORE BOOKS

*The Doctor Digs a Grave*
*The Doctor Makes a Dollhouse Call*
*The Doctor and the Dead Man's Chest*

DOCTOR JO BANKS BOOKS

*Scarecrow*

# The Doctor
# Dines in Prague

## Robin Hathaway

THOMAS DUNNE BOOKS / ST. MARTIN'S MINOTAUR

NEW YORK

THOMAS DUNNE BOOKS.
An imprint of St. Martin's Press.

THE DOCTOR DINES IN PRAGUE. Copyright © 2003 by Robin Hathaway. All rights reserved. Printed in the United States of America. No part of this book may be used or reproduced in any manner whatsoever without written permission except in the case of brief quotations embodied in critical articles or reviews. For information, address St. Martin's Press, 175 Fifth Avenue, New York, N.Y. 10010.

www.robinhathaway.com

www.minotaurbooks.com

Library of Congress Cataloging-in-Publication Data

Hathaway, Robin.
  The doctor dines in Prague / Robin Hathaway.—1st ed.
    p.   cm.
  ISBN 0-312-29036-5
  1. Fenimore, Andrew (Fictitious character)—Fiction.   2. Americans—Czech Republic—Fiction.   3. Prague (Czech Republic)—Fiction.
  4. Philadelphia (Pa.)—Fiction.   5. Kidnapping—Fiction.   6. Physicians—Fiction.   I. Title.

PS3558.A7475D625 2003
813'.54—dc21

2003046827

First Edition: November 2003

10   9   8   7   6   5   4   3   2   1

To Václav Havel,*

playwright, statesman, philosopher . . . scooter-rider

* Václav Havel was president of the Czech Republic when this book was written.

# ACKNOWLEDGMENTS

Deepest thanks to my editor, Ruth Cavin, my agent, Laura Langlie, my husband, Bob, and my daughters, Julie and Anne, for their generous advice and moral support. And special thanks to Vít Hořejš for his book, *Czechoslovak-American Puppetry*, published by GOH Productions/Seven Loaves, Inc., in 1994, and to William Keyes for his essay " 'We Were—And We Shall Be': Puppetry and Czecho-Slovak Politics, 1860–1990," and to Milan Knížák for his essay "The Marionette Proud and Dignified," both of which are included in this beautiful book.

# The Doctor
# Dines in Prague

# PROLOGUE

While going through his mail, Dr. Andrew Fenimore came across the latest issue of the *Prague Times*, which is the only Czech newspaper published in English. Fenimore subscribed to it in order to keep in touch with Prague, his mother's beloved native city. One day, he promised himself, he would brush up on his Czech and subscribe to a bona fide Czech newspaper. He had even bought some Berlitz tapes. But that day had yet to come.

As he perused the paper, a headline caught his eye:

TOWERKEEPER PLUNGES TO DEATH

The story went on to tell about the unexplained drowning of Tomas Tuk, who had guarded the tower of the Charles Bridge for over thirty years. It was his job to warn visitors of the danger of falling from the top and to make sure the tower was vacated at closing time. Apparently Mr. Tuk had fallen accidentally from the tower. There were no witnesses to his fall.

"Hmm." Fenimore stroked his chin. Odd, that a man who had guarded a tower for thirty years—and was familiar with its dangers—should have such a freak accident. Defenestration was historically a favorite murder method used in that part of the world, Fenimore recalled. There was the uprising, in 1618, when Czech Protestants tossed a whole bunch of Catholic dignitaries from a window in Prague Castle. That incident had started the Thirty Years War. And, more recently, in 1948, it was suspected that Jan Masaryk, son of Thomas Masaryk—the former president of Czechoslovakia—had been pushed from his bedroom window by Communist thugs. There was no window involved in the Towerkeeper's case—just an open archway—but the principle was the same.

Taking a pair of scissors from his desk, Fenimore clipped the article and filed it under *S*: STRANGE CASES. Crime detection was a hobby of the doctor's and his STRANGE CASES folder was overflowing.

# The Journey

And I may dine at journey's end . . .
W. B. Yeats

# CHAPTER 1

With the telephone receiver tucked under his chin, Fenimore continued packing. As he listened to the repeated staccato rings—European, not American—his anxiety rose. After a dozen rings he hung up.

He had been calling his cousin, Anna, in Prague, every day for two weeks, to no avail. He had assumed she and her family were away—at their summer cottage. But three nights ago, when he had called at four A.M.—Czech Republic time—the receiver had been lifted for a split second. No one spoke. He detected no sound of breathing. And as soon as he said, "Hello," the receiver was replaced. That was when he'd decided to go to Prague.

It seemed crazy, even to him, to take such a long trip simply because someone didn't answer the telephone. But he had a strong feeling that something was wrong—call it intuition. And he couldn't let it go. He owed it to his mother to look into it. Anna was his mother's sister's only child, and his mother and her sister had remained very close, despite the geographical distance that had separated them for all those years.

He had been in closer touch with Anna recently because her husband, Vlasta, was ill. He suffered from angina—a suffocating pressure in the center of the chest caused by too little blood getting to the heart. They had been making plans for him to come to the States for a complete cardiac evaluation. Then, suddenly, they had dropped out of sight.

Some people might wonder why Fenimore didn't notify the Prague police. This did not occur to him. Since he'd been a small child he had heard his mother's tales of the police. *The secret police.* The gestapo under the Nazis; the KGB under the Soviets. These stories had come from his mother and her family in Prague, and they had remained indelibly engraved in his mind. Despite all the noise about police brutality in the United States, the fear of the police in the States was nothing to the terror of the police in Central Europe. Although the Czechs had been free of Communism for over ten years, there had been very little retaliation—or purging of the old guard. (Czechs, by their nature, are not a vengeful people.) Some thugs from the former regime still held positions in the bureaucratic ranks. Most were probably doing a good job, but Fenimore could not bring himself to call on the Prague police for help.

Only a few things remained on the bed to be packed. A green-and-black tartan bathrobe—faded and frayed. Well, why not, after a dozen years of wear? But it was still warm, and no one ever saw him in it, except Jennifer, and she didn't care about such things. A pair of bedroom slippers, once lined with something warm and fuzzy, but now bare. And a battered shaving kit. He placed these items into the shiny new suitcase that lay open on the end of the bed. His friends had presented him with the bag the night before at an impromptu bon voyage party. His decision to go to Prague had been sudden and there had been no time to plan anything more elaborate. His good friend Detective Rafferty had brought the champagne. Mrs. Doyle, his nurse, had made the cake. Horatio, his teenage office helper (also known as Rat), had decorated the office with red and green streamers (the only ones available in Fenimore's "party drawer"). The boy had also ransacked a thrift shop and come up with an old poster of an ocean liner (although Fenimore was traveling by plane), which he had tacked on the wall. Jennifer, Fenimore's frequent companion (he refused to use the more trendy "significant other"), had organized the whole thing.

His biggest problem—getting someone to cover his patients while he was away—had been easily solved. Larry Freeman, a cardiology colleague, had offered his services as soon as he heard Fenimore's destination. But Freeman had his price: Fenimore had to take a photograph of Franz Kafka's house for him. Fenimore eagerly agreed, only to remember that he didn't own a camera. Mrs. Doyle offered to lend him her old box camera, but Jennifer bought him one of the new disposable kind. "It's lighter and easier to carry," she said. "And if you lose it you won't feel guilty for the rest of your life."

There was no denying it, the new suitcase was handsome. But much too extravagant. Fenimore would have preferred a more economical backpack. Not because he was hip or into camping out, but because he had few clothes and paid little attention to his appearance. He didn't think much of his looks. Short, middle-aged, verging on bald, with prominent ears—when confronted by his image in the mirror, he had been heard to mutter, "You certainly won't win any beauty contests."

"How do you know?" Jennifer had retorted once when overhearing him. "You have very expressive eyes, artistic hands, and a certain . . . indefinable charm."

"Humph," he said, and his ears turned bright red, which did nothing to enhance them.

The only things left on the bed were his traveler's checks, his passport, and his plane ticket. He glanced at his watch. Four-thirty. In a few minutes Jennifer would arrive to take him to the airport. Since she didn't own a car (a real city girl), they had agreed she would drive his. He had one ordeal to face before he left. As if by extrasensory perception, that ordeal sidled into the room. Sal, his marmalade cat, had sensed impending doom for three days. Now she realized it was imminent. She hopped on the bed and investigated the foreign objects lying there. Fenimore stroked her back and scratched under her chin.

"Now, don't mope," he said sternly. "You're in good hands." He had arranged for Horatio to stop by once a day to replenish her food and water and change her litter box. "I'll be back in two weeks," he assured her. "Before you can say 'Jack Robinson.'"

Her two, sharp, answering mews, Fenimore was sure, would translate into "Jack Robinson." As she leapt to the floor and wrapped herself around his ankle, the doorbell rang. Hastily disentangling himself, Fenimore picked up his suitcase and started down the stairs. With a final glance around his office and waiting room, he made for the front door. Sal was close on his heels. When he reached the vestibule, with a single adroit motion he shoved his suitcase in front of him and shut the vestibule door behind him, leaving Sal on the other side—an act that had taken years to perfect. An indignant "*Rowrrr!*" was the last sound he heard as he stepped outside.

# CHAPTER 2

"D*obré jitro,*" Jennifer greeted him with the only Czech she knew. ("Good day.")

"*Nazdar,*" he answered. (Czech for "Hello.")

They walked to the car and Fenimore shoved his bag into the trunk. She let him drive, sensing he would be happier if he had something to do.

"Got your passport?"

He nodded.

"Traveler's checks?"

"Yep."

"Plane ticket?"

He patted the breast pocket of his new navy-blue suit—the one his nurse had insisted he buy for the trip. "It's not right to show up at your cousin's, whom you've never even met, in that shabby old jacket and pants," she said, and handed him a catalog from Strawbridge's. A page was turned down at the corner, bearing a picture of the suit he was now wearing.

"Oh, here's something for you." Jennifer handed him a small parcel.

"More presents?" He tore it open. Inside was a book entitled

*Byways of Prague.* Jennifer and her father owned a bookstore specializing in rare and antique books, and she came up with an appropriate volume for every occasion. He flipped through it, glancing at pictures of bridges, churches, and castles. Would he really be seeing all these in a matter of hours?

"It's a little out-of-date," she apologized, "but it's full of juicy historical anecdotes. Did you know that Charles IV's wife could bend a sword with her bare hands?"

He entered the Expressway and headed for the airport. Ever since he could remember, his mother had shown him pictures of Prague— or "Praha," as she called it. Black-and-white or brown-and-white. Never in color. How she cherished those old picture books she had brought from home. Big, thick books she protected with mauve cloth covers stitched by her own hand. As a child, he had pored over them with her for hours, dreaming of the day when he would visit this magical city. "Not until the Communists go!" his mother would snap, and close the book. Then that sad look would come into her eyes and she would murmur, "I couldn't bear it."

He remembered the first time he had discovered she was homesick. It was opera night. His mother had brought her love of opera with her from Prague—"the city known as the Queen of Music." Unfortunately, his father didn't share her enthusiasm. And he hated to get dressed up in that "monkey suit," as he called his tuxedo. But he bore up bravely once a year for Marie's sake. On these occasions, it was his mother who held Fenimore's gaze. She piled her auburn hair on top of her head, donned a pair of diamond earrings—a wedding present from his father—and an azure velvet cloak which she fastened at her throat with an intricate silver clasp. When she kissed him good-night, her perfume was mixed with a faint hint of cedar. The cloak had been taken from its tissue paper nest in the cedar chest. He also loved her gloves. Made of soft creamy leather, he would watch her pull them on, one finger at a time, and roll them up her arm until they reached her elbow. The gloves also had a pleasant scent, but he had no words to describe it.

It was always very late when his parents returned from the opera.

Usually he was asleep. But one night he woke when they came in. He heard his father hurry up the stairs to get out of his monkey suit. But he didn't hear his mother's footsteps. She must be lingering in the hall. He slid out of bed and peered over the banister. There was only one small light on the table at the bottom of the stairs. A mirror hung above it. His mother stood there, still wearing her cloak, her auburn hair not quite as neatly arranged as when she had left earlier. A wisp of hair strayed down her cheek, giving her a girlish look. She held the opera program in one hand. As he listened, he heard her softly humming an aria. It was a familiar one. He had heard her play it often on the record player. From *Don Giovanni*. Suddenly she stopped and a strange sound came from her throat— something between a cough and a sob. She bent her head and stood that way for a moment. Then she turned and started up the stairs. Fenimore darted into his room and pretended to be asleep. Sometimes she would come in and kiss him before she went to bed. But not that night. Her footsteps passed quickly by his door without a pause. He felt uneasy. Was it possible that he and his brother and his father were not enough for her? He resolved to try to do more to make her happy. It was a long time before he fell asleep again that night.

"What are you going to do when you first arrive?" Jennifer broke in on his reverie.

"Have a bona fide Czech dinner," he answered promptly. "Schnitzel with dumplings and *palačinky* for dessert." He began to salivate at the thought.

"But you'll be arriving at nine o'clock in the morning."

"Hmm. Well, I'll have an early lunch. A párek—that's 'sausage'— on a poppy-seed roll."

"And then?"

"Then I'll check into my hotel and call Anna."

"And if there's no answer?"

He glanced at her sharply. He hadn't told anyone that he had been unable to reach his cousin. He had told everyone that he had decided on impulse to visit Prague because there was a cardiology meeting there, and he could deduct his travel expenses. "I'll keep trying until I get her."

He searched for the airport DEPARTURES sign. When he spied it, he bore left and began to look for his airline.

"There it is." Jennifer pointed to the entrance. "Wouldn't it have been better to let her know you're coming?"

He eased into the curb. "I wanted to surprise her," he lied.

Getting out, he took his suitcase from the trunk. Jennifer got out, too. They had made good time. He had an hour and a half before takeoff. Plenty of time for the security officers to do their work.

"Are you going to take her out to dinner?"

"If I can find a good restaurant. There was one my mother used to rave about. 'The Black Cat.' But I can hardly expect it to be there after sixty years."

"You never know," she said. "Things move more slowly over there. I'll park the car and wait with you."

"No." He spoke more brusquely than he intended. When he was anxious, he liked to be alone. He preferred not to talk to anyone— even Jennifer. Seeing her expression, he added hastily, "No point your wasting an hour. I have your guidebook to entertain me." He smiled.

She gave him a quick peck on the cheek and walked around to the driver's side. "Take care," she said, and drove off.

He looked after her. *"Take care"?* Why not, *"Have fun,"* or *"Bon voyage"?* Had she figured out this was not a pleasure trip? Of course she had. If it had been a pleasure trip, he would have invited her.

He turned and went inside.

# CHAPTER 3

When the flight attendant came for his drink order, Fenimore hesitated, between a martini or a ginger ale. He decided on the latter. He didn't want to arrive in Prague with his mind befuddled. It was too important. He wanted all his senses to be keen and sharp when he got off the plane: when he would first see this city he had heard so much about since he was a child and for which his mother had such a deep, abiding love.

He took *Byways of Prague* from his pocket and began to read. It opened with a short history of Czechoslovakia—beginning with the earliest settlers from the north and ending with the liberation from Germany at the end of World War II. The Communist years were left for someone else to tackle. He returned it to his pocket and stared out the window. He had been lucky to get a window seat on such short notice. They had left the East Coast behind and were high above the Atlantic Ocean. Only a few clouds were visible. Thick cotton beds floating beneath the plane, ready to catch it if anything went wrong. *Ha!* That reminded him of the fairy tales his mother used to tell him before he went to sleep. They always began in the cozy surroundings of his bedroom, but somehow ended in a spacious palace or cavernous castle in or near Prague. Were they really as splendid as she had remembered them? He glanced at his watch. In a little over eight hours he would find out.

Then he remembered why he was headed for Prague. Not to enjoy the history or to admire the architecture but to find out why his cousin, Anna, didn't answer her telephone. He began to tick off the most common reasons people don't answer their phones: (1) They weren't home. (2) They were in the shower. [For two weeks?] (3) They were home but didn't want to talk to anyone. (4) They were asleep. [For two weeks?]

Anna could be at their country cottage. He didn't have that phone number and it was unlisted. But the middle of March was an odd time to go to the country. The climate in Prague was about the same as in Philadelphia. Cold, wet, windy—full of false harbingers of spring. Sometimes it even snowed this time of year. Besides, Anna and her husband Vlasta both had jobs. They were professors at the Charles University. Anna was professor of Czech history and Vlasta headed the architecture department. During the Communist regime, they both had been relieved of their posts and forced to hold menial jobs at the post office. But, after the Velvet Revolution in 1989, when Soviet rule ended peacefully, they had been reinstated. And surely their daughter Marie (she was named after his mother) would be in school. (He calculated that she was about nine years old.) Unless she was on spring break. But what about that time his ring had been cut off—as if the receiver had been lifted and then replaced?

"Have you chosen your dinner, sir?" The flight attendant pointed to the menu card he was holding, but not reading.

"Oh . . . uh . . . I'll have the chicken breast."

"And your drink?"

"Coke, please."

She moved on to the next passenger.

As soon as the dinner trays were cleared away, many passengers pulled down their windowshades, requested pillows from the flight attendant, and tried to catch a few hours' sleep. Some continued to read, or listened to the radio with headphones, or watched the movie. Fenimore did none of these. He left his shade up and looked out into dark space. He rarely flew. His medical practice kept him homebound and he seldom attended conferences in other cities. As a result, he wasn't as casual about flying as most of his colleagues. The glimpse of the heavens outside his window thrilled him, quickening his thoughts about the nature of man and the universe. Were there other universes out there, with different life forms? If so, were those shadowy species any better than us? Less or more evil? Stuff for a science-fiction novel (that somebody had already written)?

There was no sense of motion, except when a star seemed to move. Then he remembered that it was he who was moving. "Star light, star bright, first star I see tonight . . ." But he didn't make a wish. Instead he thought about his mother. Thoughts he had not had for years. She had died when he was in medical school. No need to dwell on that. The first picture that came to him was of his mother striding along the East River Drive (now the Kelly Drive), her hair blowing in the wind. She had loved to walk, in all kinds of weather. And she always had been in good shape. In her youth she had trained in the Sokol—the Czech organization for fitness and well-being. Often she took him and his brother Richard along, but they usually had trouble keeping up with her. Sometimes they would quit and wait on a bench or lean against a tree until she returned for them—still striding, never tiring. Fenimore began to doze.

The flight attendant tapped him gently on the shoulder. Fenimore woke with a start. He had been about to dig into his favorite Czech meal—schnitzel, dumplings, and palacinky—his mother's specialty.

"Your coffee and roll, sir." The flight attendant tried to make up for her poor offering with a bright smile.

*Never mind, Fenimore. Soon you'll be able to order your favorite meal every day of the week.* "Thank you," he said. "When will we be landing?"

"In about forty-five minutes."

After a brief calculation, Fenimore adjusted his watch. They would be landing at about six A.M., Prague time.

# CHAPTER 4

To Fenimore's disappointment, at customs he had no opportunity to try out his Czech; the clerk spoke perfect English. At the end, after surreptitiously consulting his guidebook, Fenimore ventured, *"Odkud jede autobus?"*

"Over there." The clerk pointed to a bus, clearly visible through the window, parked at the curb.

Chagrined, Fenimore put his guidebook away. Before getting on the bus, he called his cousin's number from a pay phone. As usual, there was no answer.

The trip into the city was another disappointment. Row after row of gray, utilitarian apartment buildings, stretched out on either side. Constructed during the last thirty years, they were depressing reminders of the Communist era. Some even displayed graffiti. Fenimore was glad his mother couldn't see them. Turning his attention to the passengers, Fenimore strained his ears to hear some Czech spoken. But the people seated in front of him were German, those behind him were British, and the people across the aisle—who looked the most Czech—appeared to be married and had no need to talk to each other. Fenimore gave up and stared out the window at the stream of gray, nondescript buildings.

The bus driver let Fenimore off a few blocks from his cousin's apartment, in a placid suburb on the outskirts of town. It didn't look much different from some areas of West Philadelphia. There were plenty of trees, wide cement sidewalks, and trolley tracks embedded in the asphalt. As Fenimore walked, checking the house numbers, a trolley passed, clanging its bell. It sent a wave of nostalgia over him. The trolleys in Philadelphia had been replaced by buses long ago. He missed their cheerful clanging.

Anna's apartment house was also gray, but of an earlier vintage—from before the Soviet reign. Topped by a green copper roof, its tall windows were decorated with floral designs engraved in stone. When Fenimore pressed 1E, his cousin's number, there was no answering buzz. He pressed 1A, hoping to rouse the building superintendent. He was about to give up, when a harsh buzz made him jump. His nerves were not what they should be. He pushed open the door. The long hall was somber, but neat. Dark green carpeting, gray walls, and a large mirror on the right. Midway on the left, a door stood half-open. Sounds of a television came from within. Fenimore made his way toward it. As he poked his head in the door, a stout man slouched in front of the screen, glanced up. A wrestling match was in progress.

"I'm looking for Anna Borovy in one-E," Fenimore said, forgetting to use his Czech.

"Not here," the man spoke in Czech. "I haven't seen her for over two weeks."

By concentrating hard, Fenimore was able to make out "Not here" and "two weeks." He consulted his guidebook and explained in halting Czech that he was a relative who had come all the way from America and he would like to make sure she had not returned. The man, taking note of Fenimore's new suit (chalk one up for Mrs. Doyle), rose and led the way. At the end of the hall, he turned left. At the third door on the right he knocked.

Silence.

"Mrs. Borovy?"

More silence. The superintendent raised his eyebrows at Fenimore.

With a nod at the door, Fenimore indicated that he would like to go in.

With another overt appraisal of Fenimore's suit, the man drew a ring of keys from his pocket. Selecting one, he inserted it. Fenimore noticed that the man's meaty, freckled hand swallowed the key. As the door swung open, Fenimore found his heart racing. *You've been involved in too many murder mysteries,* he admonished himself. What met his eye was not a body, but a tidy living room, conservatively furnished, decorated in neutral tones of gray, beige, and brown. He stepped inside.

The super shook his head with a frown.

"It's okay." Fenimore assured him with a smile.

The man gestured at the door.

Fenimore debated. Bribery did not come easily to him. He reached for his wallet. The super's frown miraculously disappeared. Waiting until the man's footsteps had died away, Fenimore quietly closed the door. He preferred to do his snooping in private.

One wall was entirely taken up by a bookcase. A book lover by nature, Fenimore naturally gravitated toward it. Mostly hardback, academic tomes on Czech history and architecture. A few novels. One mystery—an Agatha Christie in Czech! And here, at the end of the row, a bulky manuscript. He pulled it out. Somewhat dog-eared and coffee-stained, the cover page read:

*The History of Prague*
*—People and Architecture—*
by
Vlasta and Anna Borovy

Anna had mentioned in her letters that she and her husband were coauthoring a book. Fenimore riffled though the text, pausing near the center at a thick cluster of photographs bound by a rubber band. Flipping through them, he glimpsed some of the splendid buildings of Prague. He drew out a photo of the façade of St. Vitus Cathedral. And another of the Wenceslas Chapel where the crown jewels were stored. He must visit that, he told himself—but not now. Now he had other things on his mind. He returned the manuscript to the shelf and continued his search of the apartment.

The dining room was also immaculate. Not a crumb on the carpet or a chair out of place. His mother's sister's child had inherited all the good housekeeping traits of the family. Unfortunately, they were limited to the female side. Through a narrow hallway, he continued toward the back of the apartment. He passed two doors, side by side. Behind one lay a tub, shower, and sink; behind the other—a toilet. According to European custom, the latter was separated from the rest of the bathroom.

Then he came to the master bedroom. It had a double bed, two bureaus, a large bookcase, and a straight-backed chair. A print of an abstract design hung over the bed. The top of one bureau was empty. The other had a woman's brush and comb, a china dish filled with trinkets, and two framed photographs. The largest photo was a formal grouping of the family in sepia tones. Anna, Vlasta, and Marie. Marie looked about four years old. He glanced at the smaller of the framed photos and drew a sharp breath. His mother, father, brother, and himself stared back at him in stark black-and-white tones. Fenimore had been about twelve. His brother, Richard, was ten and still shorter than Fenimore; his unexpected growth spurt didn't occur until he was in his mid-teens. Since then, Richard had towered over Fenimore. The rest of the family was smiling, but Fenimore wore a scowl. He hated to have his picture taken. It reminded him of his prominent ears.

The second bedroom was much smaller, containing a single bed, a bureau, and a small bookcase. A well-worn teddy bear lay on the bed and the lampshade was decorated with a border of dancing children. Marie's room. The beds in both rooms were neatly made-up and the curtains drawn. There was a feeling of disuse about the rooms—as if their occupants had been away for some time.

Fenimore felt shy about opening the closets. Odd for a detective—

even an amateur one. It was one thing searching a stranger's rooms. Quite another to ransack a relative's home. He forced himself to open the door of the child's closet. Several dresses hung in a row. The kind children had worn to school in the States in the 1960s, before jeans and T-shirts took over. Several pairs of jeans were folded on a shelf at the back, next to a colorful pile of T-shirts. And on the floor were three pairs of shoes. A pair of brown leather school shoes, a pair of patent-leather shoes for dress-up, and a pair of top-of-the-line sneakers. His relatives were solvent, Fenimore decided. How strange that he should measure their financial status on the basis of a pair of sneakers—shoes that had cost ten or twelve dollars when he was a boy, before Madison Avenue had elevated them to a luxury item. The closets in the master bedroom yielded nothing but the usual assortment of dresses, business suits, shoes, and sandals.

As Fenimore wandered back through the hallway, he realized he was hungry. Turning left, he passed again through the small dining room and followed a short hallway into the kitchen. For the first time, his eyes were assailed by color. A huge, ceramic stove glowed a bright yellow in one corner. It had been polished to a high gloss and its brass fixtures shone. In winter, such a large stove could probably heat most of the apartment. He ran his hand lightly over the smooth surface with pleasure. His mother had told him about these stoves. They were one of the things from her childhood that she missed. Her family had had a sea-green one, she had told him. There were two ovens. The smaller one, on the top, was used to bake delicate pastries for special occasions such as birthdays and holidays. The larger one, at the bottom, was used for baking everyday things like rolls, bread, or coffee cakes. When his mother was a girl, she used to curl up on the floor beside the stove and do her homework. "The smell of baking was such a comfort," she told him.

The thought of bread baking increased his appetite. He decided to search the kitchen—not for clues, but for food. Turning from the stove, he glanced at the kitchen counter and was startled to see a bottle of apple juice and some crackers. The bottle was half-empty and one of the crackers had a small bite out of it, as if nibbled by a mouse. He stared at the remnants of this small meal. No female member of his mother's family would ever leave half-eaten food on a kitchen counter before going out, he thought. And certainly not if she was planning to be away for two weeks!

"*Ah-choo!*"

Spinning ninety degrees, Fenimore fixed his eyes on the stove. Silence.

Had he imagined that sneeze? Keeping his eyes on the stove, he fumbled behind him for the knob of a drawer. Pulling the drawer out, he rooted inside. When he felt the sharp edge of a knife, he grabbed it. He listened a minute more, before quietly edging his way toward the stove. In a split second, this beautiful, shining purveyor of comfort and warmth had turned into a menacing monster. Knife raised and ready, Fenimore yanked open the larger oven door. Nothing happened. He bent to look inside. At first, everything looked black. Slowly, something began to take shape. A mound of old rags wedged into the space? Fenimore prodded it gently with the point of the knife.

"Ow!"

Jumping back, Fenimore watched the mound become a small figure. Slowly a pale face with two dark eyes emerged. The child in the photo!

"Marie?"

She crouched in the opening, her eyes full of fear.

"Come out," he spoke softly. "It's your cousin . . . Andrew. I won't hurt you."

She seemed unable to speak or move.

"Where are your parents?" Then he remembered: she probably didn't know English. "Where are your parents?" he repeated, in fluent Czech—and had no idea where the words came from.

Her head drooped down on her chest and she made her first sound, a harsh sob.

"My dear child." Taking hold of her hands, Fenimore gently helped her climb down from the stove.

Marie's feet had barely touched the floor before she placed her finger to her lips and hissed, "Shhh."

Fenimore looked at her in surprise. He had been racking his brain for Czech words in order to make conversation with her. What had happened to that fluent sentence he had produced a second ago? Under stress, all the vocabulary his mother had taught him seemed to be at his command. Now his mind was blank again. The human mind is a peculiar thing.

Marie ran to the back wall of the kitchen, the one that adjoined the next apartment. She touched the wall and pointed to her ears.

"Someone might hear?" Fenimore whispered, in English.

She nodded. She did know some English. *They must teach English early in the Czech schools.* He took a pen and notepad from his jacket pocket. Placing it on the counter he began to draw stick figures. A man, a woman and a little girl. He wrote names under them. *Mama. Papa. Marie.* Then he circled the *Mama* and *Papa* figures and wrote, *Kde?* ("*Where?*")

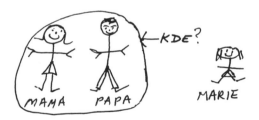

Tears filled Marie's eyes. They were beautiful Czech eyes, deep-set and brown. The warm brown of autumn leaves. Taking the pen from him, Marie drew two stick figures. Men with round heads. She added an object to the stick-hand of one of the men. A gun.

22

# CHAPTER 5

W hen?" Fenimore asked loudly, forgetting that he might be overheard.

Marie cautioned him again. Then she wrote the date—day, month, and year—European style.

The child had been living alone in this apartment on canned food and crackers for over two weeks!

Fenimore took the pen from her. Carefully, he drew a picture of a sumptuous feast—including all the delectable Czech dishes he had been dreaming of since he left Philadelphia, the land of the pretzel and the cheese steak.

Carried away, he even drew a stein of beer and wrote *Pilsner* beneath it. Hastily, he crossed it out and replaced it with an ordinary drinking glass and wrote *mléko* (*"milk"*), under it.

Marie grabbed the pen, crossed out the picture of the glass of milk, and drew a can. She wrote *COKE* on the can.

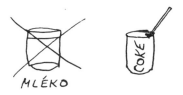

Fenimore raised his eyebrows in mock surprise.

For the first time, Marie smiled. It was the most beautiful sight Fenimore had seen since he had arrived in Prague—a city famous for beautiful sights.

"Let's go!" he whispered, reaching for her hand.

The smile vanished and she shrank back.

"What's wrong? I'll take you to a restaurant. Res-taur-ant!" he repeated. That word, at least, was almost the same in every language.

She shook her head and slapped the kitchen counter.

"Here? You want to stay here?"

She nodded.

He opened the refrigerator. Empty, except for a bottle of ketchup, half a petrified lemon, and an open can of baked beans. The cupboards revealed two cans of peas, a bag of flour, and a jar of partially crystallized honey.

Marie opened a drawer under the counter and drew out a business card. With a sly look, she gave it to him.

PIZZERIA, it read, with an address and telephone number.

Before he could stop her, she reached for the phone and began dialing. Midway, she paused. *"Sýr nebo párky?"* she asked.

*"Sýr,"* he said quickly, proud that he recognized the word for "cheese" as well as "sausage."

She redialed and ordered a large cheese pizza. It wasn't until she had hung up that Fenimore wondered if the phone was tapped. He decided not to worry about it. Exhausted from their earlier attempts at communication, they waited for the pizza to arrive in companionable silence.

The delivery boy came much faster than his American counterpart would have. He came down the back alley to the kitchen door. Marie must have instructed him to do this. Smart child. When the knock came, they both jumped. Marie ran to the door, but Fenimore stepped in front of her and peered out the window. Outside stood a boy with a bicycle, balancing a large, square cardboard box. Who else could he be? Fenimore opened the door.

"Pizza?" The boy grinned at him.

Fenimore drew several bills from his pocket, while Marie took the box. When the boy began to make change, Fenimore put up his hand. "Keep the change."

*"Děkuji,"* he said. (*"Thank you."*) The boy had understood perfectly.

When Fenimore closed the door, Marie already had opened the box and was tearing off a slice of pizza. She began shoveling it into her mouth. How long had it been since she had had a square meal? What if he hadn't come? It didn't bear thinking about. He glanced at his watch. Eleven-thirty. This was the first time he had ever had pizza before noon. Ruefully, he detached a slice for himself.

Her first slice finished, Marie opened the paper bag the boy had brought. She drew out two large red-and-white paper cups with COKE printed on the sides. She had thought of everything. She handed him a straw and poked another into the lid of her cup. As they sipped and munched, Fenimore thought, ruefully, how different his first meal in Prague was from the one he had dreamed about. . . .

# CHAPTER 6

The whole time Fenimore was eating, he was thinking—planning what to do next. He had to start looking for his cousins. And he had to start tracking down the two men with the gun. The trail was already cold. But he couldn't leave the child alone. He knew no one in Prague, except her parents: his cousins. And they obviously were not available. There was the super. But Marie had not turned to him once for help, since her parents had left. There must be a reason. . . . He was stuck.

*Brring. Brring.*

Short, staccato rings. Like gunshots. Marie and Fenimore faced the telephone as if it were a loaded gun. Fenimore moved to answer it, then thought better of it. What if it were tapped? But it might be Jennifer. He had given her the number and she had said she would call. They sat staring at the phone, listening to it ring.

When it fell silent, Fenimore grew restless. He paced the kitchen. Then he paced the apartment. He had to get moving. He had to get out of there, if only to buy food. He felt helpless. He needed help—even if it had to come from the States. He went to the phone and picked up the receiver. Replaced it and resumed pacing. His eyes roved over the living room, searching for an answer to his predicament. Books, lamps, an old-fashioned clock, a sofa, two overstuffed chairs, a desk . . . and a computer. Following his gaze, Marie came and sat down in front of the computer. She hit the mouse. The screen glowed instantly with the card faces of her most recent game of solitaire. She began to play.

*E-mail!* thought Fenimore. "E-mail!" he said aloud.

The child looked at him.

In halting Czech he asked if she could send e-mail.

With the swift touch of a few buttons, she called up the e-mail screen.

Fenimore scratched his head. What was Jennifer's e-mail address? She had mentioned it once, but since he didn't own a computer he had had no reason to remember it. He went to the phone again. This time, he dialed. Jennifer answered. At the sound of his voice, she said, "You made it!"

"What's your e-mail address?" he asked, without preamble.

"You're *not* using a computer!" She laughed.

"This is an emergency," he said shortly. "What's your address?" She gave it.

"As soon as I hang up, I'm going to send you a message. Please answer right away."

"What's wrong, Andrew?" Now she was alarmed.

"Read my message." He hung up.

Fenimore took Marie's place at the computer. Marie showed him where to type the address, then pointed him to the message space. With two fingers, he slowly began to type on the Czech-alphabet keyboard.

I need help. Marie's parents were kidnapped at gunpoint. I found her alone in the apartment, living on crackers and canned goods, hiding in the stove! I can't look for her parents or their kidnappers because I don't dare leave her alone. Please contact

Mrs. Doyle and ask her if she will come over here and baby-sit—all expenses paid. Rafferty can get her a plane reservation. Get back to me as soon as possible.

P.S. I am using e-mail because the phone may be tapped.

Helplessly, Fenimore turned to Marie who had been watching at his elbow.

She grabbed the mouse, placed the arrow on the SEND box, and clicked. The message disappeared. At last Fenimore was catching up with the electronic age.

While he anxiously waited for Jennifer's answer, Marie taught him how to play solitaire. Fenimore played while Marie kibitzed. After half an hour, he asked her to check the e-mail messages. Blank screen. Fenimore traded places with Marie and she began to play. But he didn't kibitz. He was too preoccupied.

An hour passed before they checked the mailbox again. This time there was a message.

Dear Doctor,
We're all here at the bookstore.

That explained the delay!

I've read your message and I have a suggestion. Why don't you send the child over here? I can take much better care of her where I can speak the language and I know the ropes.

Best wishes,
—Kathleen Doyle

P.S. This is Jen. If you want, I could come over and baby-sit. My passport is up-to-date and I could leave tomorrow.

P.P.S. Hi, Doc. Rat here. I'd be glad to come over. I've never been on a plane.

P.P.P.S. "Meow!" (Me, too!)

P.P.P.P.S. That was Sal.

28

Had they taken Sal to the bookstore?

Doctor—Doyle again. Don't forget to get Marie a passport.

*As if I would!*

Send plenty of warm clothes. It's still cold here even though it's almost April. And if she has a favorite toy, be sure she brings it. She may be homesick and a doll or a stuffed animal would help.

*How does Doyle know that?* Then Fenimore remembered: His nurse was from a family of eight and she had oodles of nieces and nephews.

Make a sign for her with her name on it to hold up at the airport. We don't want to miss her. We'll wait here at the bookstore until you send her plane's arrival time.

So, Doyle's "suggestion" was already a fait accompli!

P.P.P.P.P.S. I TOLD you, you should get a computer! Jen

That was all.

Fenimore typed "PASSPORT" on the e-mail screen.

Marie looked puzzled.

Frustrated, Fenimore reached for the dictionary. In Czech, passport was *pasport*. He typed, "PASPORT BUREAU."

*"Ne, ne,"* Marie said, and with a few keystrokes, took him to the Web. When *www* appeared, she typed, *czechpasportbureau.com*. After a brief pause, the Web page for the Czech Passport Bureau appeared, with instructions on how to apply in many languages: Czech, German, French, Russian, and English.

*Magic,* thought Fenimore, and cursed himself for being such a computer dunce.

He learned that in order to get a passport for Marie he must supply her birth certificate and a photograph. The latter would be easy, but the former might be hard. He read on. There was an application form and the address of the passport office in Prague. At the end was the warning: "Processing a passport takes three days."

*Three days!* Fenimore groaned.

Marie showed him how to download the application and print it out. He laid it aside and asked her to find him some U.S. airline Web sites. He found a plane that left Prague in three days. He ordered a one-way ticket and paid for it with his Visa card. He relayed this information to his friends in Philadelphia. After he had sent the message, he looked for Marie. She had vanished. He went to her room. She was lying on her bed, clutching her teddy bear.

"What's wrong?" he asked.

For answer, she rolled away from him—onto her stomach.

He went and sat on the bed. "Marie?"

She looked up, her dark eyes wet with tears. "Neodjížděj," she pleaded. ("Don't leave.")

In her distress she had reverted to Czech.

"Oh, my dear . . ." He reached for her hand. "You don't understand. *I'm* not going. You are. To America!" He grinned, sure that this news would make her happy.

She drew her hand away. *"Ne,"* she said into her pillow. "I want to stay with you."

Fenimore took a pad and pen from his pocket and began drawing. "How would you like to see this?" He showed her his crude picture of the Liberty Bell.

She shook her head.

He drew again. "How about this?" He showed her a picture of Betsy Ross hard at work on the flag.

No response.

In desperation, Fenimore reached for the bear. "What's his name?"

"Jiri." ("George.")

"Look, Jiri." He showed him both pictures. "You want to go to America, don't you?"

With a little help from Fenimore, Jiri nodded yes.

"I know what you'd like to see." Fenimore drew again.

At the sight of his relatives, Jiri clapped his paws.

Marie peered hesitantly at the picture.

"How 'bout it, Jiri?" Fenimore bounced the bear on his knee. "You can have pretzels, and cheese steaks, and ice cream—the best in the world!"

The bear jumped up and down, clapping his paws.

"But you can't leave Marie."

Jiri looked at Marie and shook his head. He touched her hand with his paw and, in a gruff, bearlike voice (which only slightly resembled Fenimore's) said, "Come on, Marie. Come with me to America!" He began jumping up and down again.

The glimmer of a smile crossed the child's face.

Fenimore placed Jiri in her arms.

She hugged him to her chest.

Fenimore asked, in his normal voice, "Is it a deal?"

She looked puzzled.

"Is it okay?"

Slowly, she nodded.

# CHAPTER 7

That hurdle over, he tackled the passport problem. "Where do Mama and Papa keep their important papers?" he asked Marie, praying she didn't say, "In the bank."

She led him into the master bedroom and pointed under the bed. He peered under and saw a strongbox. He dragged it out and blew off a thin coating of dust. It was locked.

"Key?"

She looked puzzled.

Fenimore imagined having to lug the box into a field and blow it up with a stick of dynamite. He retrieved the dictionary. "Klíč?" he said.

She brightened and led him into the kitchen. On a nail, beside the door that opened into the alley, hung a ring of keys. Fenimore had probably looked at it a dozen times since he arrived—without seeing it. Quickly, he fingered through them—door keys, car keys, closet keys, trunk keys—until he came to a small, nondescript key, cut in the shape of the letter *E*. It looked just right. He took it into the bedroom. A perfect fit. He turned it and lifted the lid of the strongbox. Inside lay a pile of legal papers wrapped in a large rubber band. A will, a document donating various organs to various organizations, three insurance policies—two life, one car—a marriage certificate, and three birth certificates. Marie's was on the bottom. "Eureka!" he cried, waving it in the air.

Marie giggled.

Hurdle number two had been scaled. Now for number three. "Photographs?" he said.

Marie led him to her mother's closet and pulled out a cardboard box. Inside were three hefty photograph albums and numerous packs of loose photos. He groaned at the thought of going through all of them. Marie reached into the box and drew out a large yellow envelope. Inside was a recent eight- by ten-inch picture of Marie and six wallet-sized pictures. They were taken at school this year, she told him.

*Praise the Lord,* thought Fenimore. He planted a kiss on top of her head and slipped two of the smaller pictures into his pocket.

Next, with Marie's help, he filled out the passport application form. It was a laborious task—communicating his questions and interpreting her answers. But, with the aid of the dictionary, they got through it. He had taken the precaution of writing it in pencil first, then inking it over. When it was finished, Fenimore sat back with a sigh and looked at his watch. Good grief! All this passport baloney had taken almost three hours! It was two-thirty; the passport office closed at four o'clock, and it was on the other side of town.

An unpleasant thought struck him. What if someone was watching the apartment? If the phone was being tapped, the apartment might also be under surveillance. No one must know that Marie was here. But the government never would issue her a passport without seeing her in person. Somehow he had to smuggle her out. But how?

"I'm hungry!" Marie handed the pizzeria card to Fenimore.

His stomach contracted. He glanced at his watch. Almost three! But the last thing he wanted was a pizza. As he stared at the card, slowly his grimace reshaped itself into a broad grin. "Can you ride a bicycle?" he asked.

Puzzled, she nodded.

*Poor kid probably thinks I've flipped,* thought Fenimore. With the help of the dictionary and a few awkward sketches, he outlined his plan.

Milo, the pizza delivery boy, was more than happy to help out. Their pizza had been the last delivery of his shift. For ten dollars, all he had to do was lend his white cap, his jacket, and his bicycle to Marie, and stay in the apartment playing video games for two hours—about the time it would take them to go to the passport office, do their business, and return. The jacket was too big for Marie, but with a sweatshirt underneath it didn't look too bad. Her jeans and sneakers were much the same as the boy's. But she had to do something with her hair. It was shoulder-length. Marie solved the problem by pulling it back into a ponytail and tucking it up under the cap. Fenimore inspected her closely. A bit young to be delivering pizza, but she would ride by in a flash, and since the spy would not be looking for a pizza delivery boy, they probably wouldn't give her a second glance.

The plan was for Fenimore to leave first, by the front door. Go to the pay phone at the corner and call a taxi. When the taxi arrived, Fenimore would call the apartment, let the phone ring twice and hang up. That was the signal for Marie to leave by the back door, ride the bike down the alley and around the corner to where he would be waiting. Fenimore would store the pizza uniform in a shopping bag and they would take the cab to the passport office. But, what about the bike? They couldn't leave it on the curb. Prague, like any big city, had petty thieves. Fenimore decided that ten minutes after Marie left, Milo should leave by the back door, stroll around the corner, and pick up his bike. Then he would ride it back to the apartment and park it in the alley. Fenimore found the key to the back door on the ring of keys, detached it, and gave it to Milo. Fenimore checked to make sure he had everything: passport application, birth certificate, photos, and shopping bag. Before leaving, he looked down the alley one last time. It was empty, except for a line of dark-green trash cans.

· · ·

Everything went according to plan. There was no trouble at the passport office, either. By the time Fenimore and Marie returned home, it was dark, and Fenimore thought it was safe to let the cab drop them at the entrance to the alley. When they knocked at the back door, Milo, immersed in his video game, took a while to answer. After the third knock, the boy came to the door. Fenimore was a nervous wreck. But he gave the boy his ten dollars in korunas, thanked him for his help, and ordered a *sýr* pizza to be delivered at noon the next day.

Exhausted, Fenimore fell asleep on the couch early, but Marie—excited after her first day out in over two weeks—stayed up, playing solitaire late into the night.

# CHAPTER 8

Fenimore woke early, feeling refreshed. Marie slept on. This gave him some time to work out the breakfast problem. He had not gone to the store yesterday for several reasons. First, his time had been taken up with passport drivel; second, he was afraid to leave Marie home alone and he was also afraid to take her with him. Either one was risky. And he couldn't ask Milo to come to their rescue again. And the thought of pizza for breakfast made his stomach lurch. He opened the kitchen cabinets one by one, scanning their meager contents. A giggle interrupted him. Marie stood in the doorway, staring at his legs. He looked down. All he had on was his long johns. He had removed his trousers the night before to avoid wrinkling them. After all, they were brand new.

"In America, this is what everyone wears to bed," he told her with a straight face. "Here." He took out the flour and sugar and made stirring motions with his hand, indicating she should find him a bowl and spoon.

Marie quickly produced both, and a measuring cup as well. Her cheeks were flushed, her eyes bright. A night's sleep in her own bed had done wonders for her. She had told Fenimore that she had slept in the oven on a pile of towels every night, because she had been afraid the man with the gun would come back.

He carefully measured two cups of flour, one cup of sugar, and one and a half cups of water into the bowl. While Marie stirred this concoction, he searched for a skillet. He found one, but nothing to grease it with. How would he keep the pancakes from sticking? He solved this by making one giant pancake and sliding the spatula under it every few seconds. When it was done on one side—to Marie's delight—he flipped it in the air. When it was brown on both sides, Fenimore cut the pancake, serving each of them half. Marie took a bite and made a face. Fenimore also grimaced. He grabbed the jar of crystallized honey from the cabinet and spread a gob on each half. A far cry from maple syrup, but "beggars can't be choosers," as his grandmother used to say. Fenimore could only manage to eat two-thirds of his. Marie ate all of hers. She still must have been starving.

Once the dishes were done (all two of them), it was only nine o'clock. Three long days stretched before him until it was time to take Marie to the airport. How would he get through them, knowing that he should be searching for his cousins? Perhaps he could use the time to get more information from Marie. Maybe she knew more than she *knew* she knew. If that made sense. There were so many questions: What did the men look like? What were they wearing? How did they come? Why hadn't she asked the super for help? Why did she think the walls had ears? And, most important, why would anyone want to kidnap her parents?

He decided to find out. But, because of the language barrier, it would not be easy. He would have to be inventive; turn it into a game. Armed with a pad, pen, and the thick Czech-English dictionary, he began his gentle interrogation. Laboriously, Fenimore looked up words and wrote them down, trying to compose his questions. After watching him struggle for a few minutes, Marie ran into her room and came back with a big, brightly colored picture book. *Oh, no,* thought Fenimore, *she's bored already and wants me to read to her.* He recognized the style of the pictures right away. They were by a famous American illustrator—Richard Scarry. He had often read Scarry's books to his niece and nephew in Philadelphia. But this book was different. It wasn't just a picture book—it was a *pictionary*. The book was divided into sections with subtitles such as "Food," "Clothing," "Transportation," "Body Parts," et cetera. Under each heading were pictures of the appropriate objects. But, most importantly, under each object was listed its name—not in one, but in four languages: German, French, English, and Czech! Fenimore grabbed the book and let out a whoop. If Mr. Scarry had walked in at that moment, Fenimore would have hugged him.

Pointing to a picture of a loaf of bread, he read the foreign names under it to Marie, careful to use the proper accent for each: "*Das Brot . . . le pain . . .* bread . . . *chleb*."

Marie disappeared into her room again. This time she came back carrying Jiri. She didn't want the bear to miss all the fun. During his questioning, Fenimore included the bear. After asking Marie a question, he would turn to Jiri and whisper in his ear. Then he would lift Jiri up to his own ear, so the bear could whisper something into it. After listening for a minute, Fenimore would raise his eyebrows, gasp, and look horrified. Marie would double over with laughter.

Slowly the game wore on, interrupted only for meals, when Fenimore gritted his teeth and ordered another pizza. One benefit of eating pizza was that they came to know Milo. If their pizza was his last delivery of the day, he stayed awhile and joined in their game. His English was more advanced than Marie's and he served as their interpreter. "But," he informed them, "I like video games better."

On the second day, when Milo delivered their lunch, Fenimore struck a deal with him. He could play video games if he would stay with Marie, while Fenimore made a quick trip to the store. For the first time since Fenimore had arrived, they had a decent dinner. Unfortunately, it included no Czech delicacies. Fenimore only knew how to cook American style. The meal consisted of roast chicken, mashed potatoes, peas, and chocolate pudding. For the beverage, he insisted that Marie drink milk instead of soda. Fenimore drank milk, too—to set a good example.

By the end of the second day, Fenimore had learned the following.

1. The two kidnappers were young men and had come on *motocykly* (motorcycles). Marie had heard them pull up outside.
2. They wore *kožená bunda* (leather jackets).
3. They were *špinavy* (dirty).

"Like me?" Fenimore suddenly realized he hadn't taken a shower since he had arrived.

"*Ne*," she giggled.

4. They spoke Czech with a funny accent.

"Russian?"
She shrugged.
"German?"
She shrugged again.

5. The super was *spatny* (bad).

Marie screwed up her face.

Fenimore knew what *spatny* meant. His mother had used it to refer to him often, when he was a boy. But he wasn't satisfied. He wanted to know *how* the super was bad. Was he *(a)* disagreeable? *(b)* dishonest? *(c)* violent? Some things could not be described with pictures. He found himself acting out each of these categories in the manner of charades. For "disagreeable," he frowned and stuck out his tongue at Jiri. Marie laughed, but shook her head. For "dishonest," Fenimore put his wallet in Jiri's lap, snuck up behind him, snatched it, and slipped it inside his own jacket pocket. "*Ne, ne, ne!*" Marie laughed again. But when, in an attempt to illustrate violence, Fenimore took Jiri across his knee and playfully spanked him, Marie did not laugh. She grabbed the teddy bear from him and clutched him to her chest. The look of fear in her eyes was the same as on the day Fenimore had found her. Remembering the super's thick, freckled hand, he wondered if he had ever touched her. Fenimore decided that he had learned all he could from Marie. He let her return to the computer and her games of solitaire.

That night, before Marie fell asleep, Fenimore came into her room and sat on her bed. Instead of reading her a bedtime story, he told her about his friends in Philadelphia. Again, he resorted to drawings. (If the medical profession ever became intolerable, he could always switch to art, he thought.) There they were, all in a row. . . .

Mrs. Doyle   Horatio (Rat)   Jennifer   Sal

Marie was especially taken with Sal. *"Kočka"* she asked. (*"Cat?"*) Fenimore's artistic attempt was somewhat ambiguous.

He nodded.

"I like *kočky*," she said, with a wicked grin.

Fenimore sent a silent prayer across the Atlantic, begging Sal's forgiveness.

They had showered, dressed, and checked the contents of Marie's suitcase for the last time. The plan was the same as three days ago when they had gone to the passport office.

At ten-thirty sharp, Milo knocked on the door. Fenimore let him in and looked down the alley to make sure the coast was clear.

A truck was parked in the alley and some unloading was going on. Marie peered out, too, and turned pale.

"What's wrong?"

She shook her head.

"There's plenty of room. You can slip past—"

"*Ne!*" She ran into her room and shut the door.

As Fenimore stared down the alley, he caught sight of the super reaching up from the basement entrance to receive a box.

Fenimore looked at his watch. Ten forty-five. The plane left at two. And they had to pick up her passport. He knocked on her door. "Marie. . . ."

"*Ne!*" she shouted.

He went and stood behind Milo. Immersed in his game, the boy was unaware of his predicament. Fenimore watched the green-and-yellow gnomes zigzagging across the screen for a while. Then he went back to the kitchen and looked down the alley. The truck was gone. There was no sign of the super. He called to Marie. Cautiously, she came out of her room. He helped her into Milo's uniform and repeated the instructions of two days ago. Pocketing the ring of keys, he left by the front door.

Because of the time lost, Fenimore ordered the cabbie to drive *rychlý* (fast). Although Marie's spirits had been high while they were preparing to leave, the truck incident had put a damper on them. In the taxi, she was subdued. Now that she was actually on her way, Fenimore felt her anxiety building. After all, she had probably never traveled alone before. She huddled in the corner of the taxi, clutching Jiri. Fenimore directed his conversation mainly to the bear. In halting Czech he told him about all the wonderful things he would see in Philadelphia. Besides his relatives at the zoo, there was the Franklin Institute and Independence Hall. The "Rocky" statue and lobsters at Bookbinders. From time to time, Fenimore glanced out the back window to see if they were being tailed. But there was no sign of any car sticking to them. The passport was ready when they arrived and the rest of the trip was uneventful.

Once inside the airport terminal, Fenimore tucked Marie's passport into a cloth purse he had found in his cousin's bureau, and added some U.S. currency—two twenties and some coins. He pinned the purse to the inside of her jacket with two giant safety pins. "Keep your passport in there at all times," he told her sternly. "Don't show it to anyone except the man in the window here," he pointed to the airport official checking people's passports, "and the man in the window in Philadelphia. You understand?"

She nodded.

He prayed that she did.

Last night, while Marie was sleeping, Fenimore had made a small passport for the bear—out of cardboard—and drawn his picture inside. When it was their turn to step up to the window and show Marie's passport, Fenimore pulled out Jiri's, too. He hoped the official had a sense of humor. The clerk's eyebrows shot up. He looked from the bear to Marie. Without a word, he stamped the little passport. Marie's smile was his reward.

After customs, there was a half-hour wait before boarding. Fenimore thought Marie should have something to eat. First he checked the restaurant area for suspicious-looking characters. All seemed clear. He headed toward an attractive café that promised coffee, hot chocolate, and some succulent Czech pastries. He was beginning to salivate when he felt a tug on his arm. "Look, Uncle Andrew!" Marie pointed to a red awning decorated with two golden arches. Reluctantly, he changed his direction.

At the barrier, Fenimore briefed the flight attendant, who spoke Czech and English, about who was meeting Marie. She assured him that Marie would be given safe conduct to his friends in Philadelphia. He reminded Marie about the sign in her suitcase, to be sure to take it out when she reached the other airport, and to hold it up high. He gave her a peck on the cheek and Jiri a pat on the head. As Marie headed down the ramp, she turned twice to wave. The second time she raised Jiri's paw. Then they disappeared.

Fenimore swallowed three times and was amazed to find the lump was still there. He headed for the nearest bar. Not even a Pilsner helped. He ordered another. He needed to get his bearings. He was not a chameleon. Switching from nanny to detective would take a little time.

He let his mind idle, watching the people rove to and fro through the airport. The crowd was not as varied as in the Philadelphia airport. Here, everyone looked pretty much the same. The same color, the same demeanor, the same economic background. And they were quieter. Missing was the occasional raucous outcry or sudden belly laugh. No doubt about it, Czechs were more withdrawn and subdued than Americans. But, not long ago, they had been ruled by an oppressive Communist regime. Such a regime did not encourage freedom of expression—or hilarity. The Czechs were not chameleons, either. It would take time.

Leaving the bar, Fenimore stopped an airport official to ask where he could buy a bus ticket into the city. He had decided on his next step—to go to the Charles University and talk to his cousins' colleagues. Maybe one of them could throw some light on the kidnapping. As Fenimore climbed onto the bus, it dawned on him that he was free. Being trapped in that apartment caring for a child for three days had weighed on him more than he realized. Despite the heavy responsibility that still lay before him—the rescue of his cousins—he felt a lightness of being.

# The City

Prague—a precious jewel in the country's crown of stone.
Goethe

# CHAPTER 9

Once on the bus, Fenimore immersed himself in his guidebook. The Charles University was founded in the 1300s by the emperor Charles IV and modeled after the Sorbonne in Paris—"so that the Czechs did not need to beg for the crumbs of learning abroad but found at home a laden table," the book quoted the emperor.

It was the oldest university in Central Europe. His mother had graduated first in her class from the Teachers' College, a great achievement in the 1940s. Then she had been given a teaching post. His father was American and had met her at the end of World War Two when he was stationed briefly in Prague. Captivated by this brilliant, auburn-haired beauty, he proposed after only a few weeks. Equally enamored, she accepted. The plan was for him to return to Philadelphia, establish his medical practice, and then send for her. (People were more conservative in those days.) But shortly after he returned to the States, the Communists took over Czechoslovakia, adopting Prague as their headquarters. Members of the Czech faculty and students were forced from the University and made to work in factories and mines. Those were the lucky ones. Others were beaten, imprisoned, and even killed. His mother's letters to his father became more and more desperate. He sent her money and, with the help of friends, she escaped to France. When she arrived in Philadelphia, she and his father were married the same day in a civil ceremony, at City Hall.

His mother had no desire to teach in America. "My English will never be good enough," she said. The women's movement had not yet begun and she was under no pressure to work outside the home. She was content to look after her husband and two sons—cooking, sewing, gardening. In her spare time, she took advantage of Philadelphia's cultural opportunities, of which there were many. The Philadelphia Orchestra at the Academy of Music, under Eugene Ormandy, was universally acknowledged as the best in the world. There was the theater—the Walnut, the Locust, the Forrest, the Shubert—and the opera several times a year. And many art museums. Her favorite was the Rodin Museum. Within walking distance of their Spruce Street town house ("walking distance," by his mother's standards), she would go there and sit for hours—especially in the spring when the tall French doors were thrown open and the cherry trees bloomed in the garden. It reminded her of Praha, she said. Sometimes she would take Fenimore and his brother along—and after they had dutifully admired the statue of Balzac, and she, *The Kiss*—she would take them to Fairmount Park to play.

He searched his guidebook for more information about the University.

A well of mineral water, from which fourteenth-century students quenched their thirst, still holds a place in the reception hall. And the timbers in the ceiling—half a meter (nearly two feet) in diameter—are reminders of the great forests that surrounded the city long ago. The black marble floor shines like a lake in the moonlight.

Fenimore tucked the book into his jacket pocket and prepared to meet his cousins' colleagues—all learned professors at this venerable university. In Central Europe, a professor is a revered personage, not an object of faint ridicule (sometimes labeled "absentminded"), as in America.

Absorbed in his thoughts, Fenimore descended the bus. When he raised his eyes, his first sight of the city struck him with the impact of a physical blow. Before him rose a panorama of bridge, castle, and cathedral—in Technicolor! Fenimore had seen this view many times, but always in the muted, sepia tones of his mother's old picture books. In the late-afternoon sun, it glowed with the warmth of rich gold. He stood riveted—staring, until a passerby inquired, *"Zatril jstese?"* (*"Lost?"*)

Fenimore shook his head and moved on. Although his feet were drawn toward the Charles Bridge and the castle, conscious of his obligation, he turned resolutely toward the University.

The entrance to the University was a disappointment. A utilitarian building constructed of ordinary blond brick, vintage 1950s. Where were the medieval stone walls that soared to a ceiling of thick, ancient beams and the black marble floor that shone like a lake in the moonlight? CLOSED. UNDER CONSTRUCTION, a sign read.

Because of the spring break, the prosaic reception area was empty and silent, missing the usual noisy bustle of students. The only human being in sight was a stubby man in workclothes pushing a broom in a desultory manner over the dusty wood floor.

"I'm looking for the dean," Fenimore said in Czech. (He had prepared this statement the night before with the aid of his dictionary.)

"Nobody here. Closed for vacation."

Fenimore's heart sank. "Nobody?" he repeated in disbelief.

With a smile the man shook his head, taking pleasure in repeating the bad news.

Refusing to believe that such a vast university could be completely empty, Fenimore headed for the stairs.

"Halt!"

Pausing, Fenimore adopted a desperate expression and said, "Toilet?"

The man's face relaxed and he gave directions to a washroom on the second floor.

On the second floor, a long corridor confronted Fenimore with a string of closed doors. He began systematically to open them and poke his head inside. Room after room revealed row upon row of empty desks, a blackboard, and that ripe odor of unwashed students that lingers in centers of learning throughout the world. Persisting, Fenimore climbed the stairs to the third floor. Here he found most of the doors locked. Those that were unlocked, opened into small offices, probably belonging to faculty members. By American standards, they were meagerly furnished with only the basics—a desk, a chair, and a bookcase—all in shabby condition. About to give up, Fenimore opened a door at the end of the hall.

A slight man with a goatee and wire-rimmed glasses glanced up, startled.

"Excuse me," Fenimore apologized. "Can you help me?"

"*Američan?*"

Fenimore nodded sheepishly, ashamed that his American accent was so obvious.

"Jan Redik." The man rose and offered his hand. "What can I do for you?" His English was perfect.

"Andrew Fenimore. Cardiologist." He mentioned his credentials only because in Prague he knew they would inspire respect and he needed all the respect he could get.

The professor's nod bordered on a bow.

"I am looking for my cousins—Professors Anna and Vlasta Borovy." Did he detect a slight intake of breath? "Do you know them?"

"Of course." He nodded.

Not wanting to elaborate further, Fenimore said, "I came to Prague unexpectedly. I had no time to let them know, and I haven't been able to locate them. I wondered if they had mentioned any special vacation plans. . . ."

The man shook his head. "We are only colleagues. They would not have confided their plans to me." He spoke rapidly and Fenimore detected a faint whiff of academic politics.

The man began packing up his books and papers, preparing to leave.

"Would you happen to know any friends of theirs who I might contact?"

He paused in his packing and frowned. "Ah . . ." He suddenly brightened. "Ilsa Tanaček. She would know. Come." Stuffing the remaining papers into his briefcase, he picked up his books and grabbed a shabby parka from a peg on the wall. Locking the door behind him, he led Fenimore to an old-fashioned pay phone tucked in a niche at the end of the hall. In America, every professor would have his own telephone—and probably a cell phone as well. Fenimore waited while Redik placed the call and spoke to someone in rapid Czech. Fenimore did not even attempt to follow his words. Finally the professor turned. "She will speak to you," he said.

When Fenimore took the receiver, he was relieved to hear a woman's voice speaking in English, with only a slight accent. He explained his problem. The voice suggested they meet for coffee, and named a café near the University. To identify himself, Fenimore told her he would be carrying a small blue book titled *Byways of Prague.*

The woman laughed heartily. "And I will be wearing a big red rose!"

After thanking Professor Redik profusely, Fenimore hurried from the building. *At last, I'm getting somewhere,* he told himself. The thought lent wings to his feet.

# CHAPTER 10

Ilsa Tanacek was not wearing a big red rose, but she resembled one. She was a large blonde woman with a rosy face. Seated by the window at the front of the café, she spotted Fenimore immediately. Carrying his blue book before him like a flag, he entered the cozy café. With a big smile, she waved him over to her table.

Before he could finish his halting thanks, she interrupted : "We are very good friends, Anna and I, but we see so much of each other during the academic year, we don't usually keep in touch over the holidays. You are worried about her?"

"Not exactly," he said cautiously. "You see, I arrived unexpectedly. I would just like to find them."

Behind her cordial expression, the woman's gray eyes were keen. "Why are you worried?" she persisted.

"They have been missing for over two weeks," he blurted.

"Missing?" Her eyes narrowed.

Relying on his instincts about people, Fenimore decided to risk the truth. In low, measured tones, he told Ilsa everything Marie had told him about her parents' abduction. Ilsa did not react as an American would—with stunned horror. And she did not ask the obvious question, *Have you contacted the police?* She was Czech. Abductions had been a frequent practice under the Communists and she understood exactly why he had not involved the police. Fenimore ordered coffee and it arrived before she spoke again. To his disappointment, what she said seemed to have no bearing on what he had just told her.

"Have you been to Mala Strana?" she asked, rather loudly.

"No."

"Oh, you must see it. I will give you a personal tour."

Puzzled, Fenimore nodded. He had hoped for more than the offer of a tour. As they sipped their coffee Ilsa rattled on about other famous tourist sites in Prague. How it was not a good time to visit because of the weather, but he must make the best of it. There were many indoor amusements. The opera, the symphony, the theater. Her face glowed with pride. On and on she went about "the new Prague." The post–Velvet Revolution Prague. The Václav Havel Prague. She waxed especially eloquent about the president: "What a statesman! What a philosopher! What a scooter-rider . . ."

"Excuse me?" asked Fenimore.

"When he was first elected, President Havel was so overcome by the size of the Hrad, or castle, where his office is located, that he rode a scooter to help him get from one meeting to another." She smiled. "The old guard was scandalized." She laughed the hearty laugh that had won her over to Fenimore on the telephone. Then she glanced at her watch. "Have you had dinner?"

Fenimore grinned wryly. "My total consumption of food today has been half a pancake and a slice of pizza."

"Come with me." She rose.

As he followed her, he noticed that, despite her bulk, Ilsa maneuvered a path between the crowded tables with an easy grace.

# CHAPTER 11

While they had been in the coffee shop, dusk had fallen. The windows of the passing trams glowed a warm yellow, and in the distance, the statues on the Charles Bridge were illuminated by the bluish flicker of gas lamps. For a moment Fenimore forgot his mission, falling under the spell of the ancient city at twilight.

"We will cross Karlovy Most, the Charles Bridge, to Malá Strana, or Lesser Town," she translated for him. "I know a restaurant where we can talk without fear of being overheard." Ilsa brought him back to reality.

They crossed the busy avenue and shouldered their way through the crowd toward the Old Bridge Tower. Black with age, the square structure was decorated with sculpture and shields bearing inscriptions that he would have liked to read, but which were impossible to make out in the fading light. To the right of the tower, one statue stood apart from the rest. Fenimore recognized it immediately: the emperor Charles IV—benevolent ruler of Bohemia and Prague, builder of this ancient bridge which bore his name. Fenimore felt a little dizzy with the realization that he was really in Prague—or "Praha," as his mother had called it.

In his mother's picture books, the Charles Bridge had always been half empty, occupied by a handful of strollers. This evening it was thick with vendors, artists, musicians, and tourists.

Ilsa apologized. "It is always like this now, except at four o'clock in the morning. Tourists! *Phttt!*" Then, remembering that Fenimore fell into this category, she covered her embarrassment by asking, "Would you like to go up the tower?" Without waiting for an answer, she pulled the door open for him.

The steep steps followed the curve of the tower. Now and then they paused to catch their breath and peer through the narrow slits from which archers had shot their arrows centuries ago. At the top of the staircase, loomed a solitary, stone figure.

"The guard." Ilsa giggled. "Look, he's wearing skirts."

And so he was. His naked calves were visible in the rear, but the rest of him was nothing to giggle about. He crouched above them, his expression menacing enough to daunt the bravest tourist. But not Ilsa. She pushed past the statue to a small wooden door that opened with a creak. They stepped onto a narrow path that circled the cone-shaped copper roof. The only protection from falling to the river below was a slender iron railing. Fenimore remembered the man he had read about in the *Prague Times*. The human tower guard—Tomas Tuk—who had fallen over the railing and drowned. The name had stayed with Fenimore because one of his favorite nursery rhymes had been about a fellow named Tommy Tucker who sang for his supper. *It wouldn't take much to push a man over that railing*, he thought.

Keeping well away from the railing, Fenimore took in the vast panorama of roofs, steeples, and domes—their sharp edges blunted in the twilight. The vista stretched as far as the eye could see . . . Charles IV's vision in the 1300s now a reality. And now, after hundreds of years of bondage, the city was free again. Only once before had Czechoslovakia tasted such freedom. Between the two World Wars, when Thomas Masaryk was president and the country had won her independence from the Austro-Hungarian Empire. Those had been her happiest years, when she was free, prosperous, and united. Until the Nazis came, and after that—the Communists.

Ilsa touched his arm. "Shall we go?"

He shook his head—not in refusal, but to bring himself back to the present. As Fenimore passed the stone keeper of the tower, he waved him a mock farewell.

As they crossed the bridge, Ilsa told him, "Thousands of eggs were sent by farmers from all over the country and mixed with the mortar to form a binder. That's why this bridge has lasted over a thousand years. One farmer sent hard-boiled eggs 'because they would travel better.' " She laughed. Drawing his attention to a wall on the far bank, she said, "That's the Bread Wall. At one time during Charles's reign the people were very poor. Too poor even to buy bread. The good king created a project for them. He had them build that wall, even though there was no need for it, and paid them not with money, but with bread and shoes for their families. Sometimes it's called 'the Hungry Wall.' "

Fenimore remembered the legend well. His mother had told it to him often. Once his father, overhearing her, had muttered sardonically, "The first WPA project."

Passing the many statues of heroes and saints on the bridge, Ilsa paused before only one. Actually, it wasn't even *on* the bridge, but on a pedestal below it. They had to lean over the bridge wall to see it. "I'd like you to meet Bruncvik." She introduced Fenimore to the statue.

It was of a youth in full armor, carrying a sword.

"He is our 'Roland,' " she explained. "A knight so brave, a lion befriended him. See the lion in his coat-of-arms?" She pointed.

Peering through the dusk, Fenimore could barely make out a lion engraved in a corner of his shield.

"According to legend, this knight's real sword is buried in the bridge wall and during Prague's darkest hour, it will burst forth and save the city."

"I thought Prague had had her darkest hour . . . during World War Two. Don't tell me she's scheduled for another?"

Ignoring this, she led him through the archway of a second, smaller tower and they stepped into Malá Strana, Lesser Town, one of the oldest sections of Prague. Here, instead of broad avenues and large buildings, the streets were narrow and crooked, crowded with small houses and shops. As they walked, the gas lamps cast their shadows on the walls and cobblestones. Although enchanted by the setting, Fenimore's stomach was beginning to grumble. "Where is this restaurant?" he asked plaintively. He could almost taste the schnitzel, dumplings, and *palačinky* like his mother used to make.

"Around the next bend." Ilsa quickened her steps and stopped abruptly before a white sign decorated with Asian characters. A smaller sign below read, THAI RESTAURANT, for the benefit of American tourists.

Swallowing his disappointment, Fenimore followed Ilsa inside.

But he understood her choice. The restaurant was nearly empty and the walls were lined with booths where they could talk in complete privacy. They slid into a booth near the back and began to study the menus. While they waited for their order, Fenimore took advantage of the seclusion. "Did my cousins seem unusually anxious or worried recently?" he asked.

Ilsa thought a minute and shook her head. "Nothing out of the ordinary. We are all anxious and worried at the end of term. The crush of reading papers and getting grades in on time is always nerve-racking."

"Did they mention anything about going away?"

She considered. "No. In fact, I remember Anna saying they were going to stay home and try to finish their book."

"The book on architecture?"

"You know about that?"

"I found the manuscript in their bookcase when I was looking for some clue to their disappearance."

Ilsa gazed at him intently. "The deadline is this summer. They've been working on it for years. They had to keep it secret under the Communists, but now . . . It is hard to finish anything when you teach full-time."

"The voice of experience?"

She nodded.

"What are you working on?"

"Medieval manuscripts. I spend all my spare time at the Strahov Library."

"You professors are an industrious lot."

"We are so happy to be free at last to pursue our life's work. Under the Communists our hands were tied. It was so frustrating."

"Can you think why anyone would want to kidnap Anna and her husband?"

Ilsa frowned. "Ransom is the usual reason. But there was no note?"

"No."

"Besides, the Borovys aren't rich . . . and if they were, the kidnappers would have taken their child, not the parents."

"Perhaps they were after Marie, but when they couldn't find her, they settled for her parents."

Ilsa shook her head. "It doesn't make sense."

"I agree." Fenimore sighed. "Do Anna and Vlasta have any other friends I could talk to?"

"Everyone's away. Most professors travel during spring break, either into the countryside or abroad."

The waitress brought their meal, which they ate in silence. Fenimore had trouble swallowing his fortune cookie. Such a poor substitute for *palačinky*. His fortune wasn't very good, either. "Everything comes to him who waits," it read. "What's yours?" he asked Ilsa.

"Romance with a foreigner." Laughing, she cast him a coquettish glance and tossed it in her tote bag.

Fenimore felt his ears blush.

As they left the restaurant, Fenimore paused before a shop window with a display of marionettes.

Ilsa, who had gone ahead, turned back. "You like them?"

Fenimore was entranced.

She led him inside. Every niche and cranny was crowded with puppets: kings and queens, princes and princesses, wizards and witches, jugglers and jesters. Even Hollywood was represented, in the forms of Charlie Chaplin and Groucho Marx. The faces were what intrigued Fenimore. Hand-carved from wood, each one had its own unique expression. And the eyes, although painted, seemed to shift and wink in the dim light of the shop.

"May I help you?" The proprietress spoke to him in English. How did they know? His mother had always told him he looked Czech, with his deep-set eyes and aquiline nose.

"Fantastic," he murmured.

"Yes. The Czech puppets are famous," Ilsa said. "These are made by different artists from all over the Czech Republic and Slovakia. If you look closely, you will notice that each group has a slightly different style."

"That's correct," said the shopkeeper, and pointed to the signs below each group of marionettes bearing the name of their artist.

"And what handsome costumes! Silk, satin, velvet, and fur. So perfect." Ilsa gently ran her finger over the ermine collar of one marionette that bore a strong resemblance to the emperor Charles IV. His gold crown was studded with pasteboard jewels. The artist had even captured the former ruler's benevolent expression.

Ilsa and the shopkeeper chatted while Fenimore enjoyed the marionettes on his own. As he gazed at them, dangling limply from their strings—their painted faces stiff and staring—he imagined them leaping and laughing, singing, and dancing, after the shop closed. He had to have one. He would buy one—for Marie, of course. But which one? They were all wonderful. Should he close his eyes and take the first one he touched? No. One seemed to be looking at him more plaintively than the others. The jester. His silvery satin suit was decorated with scarlet pom-poms and his jaunty scarlet cap bore a silver bell at the tip. His smooth, pale face was accented with red at the cheekbones and his rouged mouth turned up slightly at the corners. His eyes were the only sad note. Larger than life, they reflected the sadness behind most jests. Like a puppy in a pet shop, Fenimore could almost hear the marionette pleading, *Take me home. Take me home.* He reached out and lifted the jester from his peg.

"Ah," Ilsa expressed her approval. "Kasparek, the clown."

"For my little cousin," Fenimore explained.

"Of course." She nodded knowingly.

The shopkeeper wrapped the marionette in tissue paper, carefully separating the strings so they wouldn't become tangled, before tucking him in a box.

"Marie will love her gift," Ilsa said with a twinkle, as they left the shop.

"Hmm." At the mention of his cousin, Fenimore glanced at his watch. "I'd better go home and check my e-mail," he said, "and find out if she arrived safely."

"You don't have to go home to do that."

"What do you mean?"

"We have cyberstations right here in town. Look, there's one." She pointed to a red-and-blue neon sign: CYBER CAFE. "They rent computer time. For a small fee they'll set you up online."

"I'll be damned." Fenimore was impressed.

"We are very up-to-date these days in Praha."

A voice informed him in Czech, *"You have mail,"* and a succinct message followed.

> Marie and Jiri arrived safely.
> Love, J, D, H, M, Jiri, and Sal.

As Fenimore entered Jennifer's e-mail address, Ilsa peered over his shoulder, lending encouragement.

With one finger he awkwardly typed, *Message received.* (Mrs. Doyle did all the typing in his office.)

> Love to all,
> F.

When Fenimore signed off, Ilsa said, "Shall we have a drink to celebrate?"

Surprised by a slight tingle where she touched his arm, he followed her eagerly across the street to the lighted café.

# CHAPTER 12

Fenimore woke with a slight hangover. The beer had been good, but even the best beer can have ill effects if you overdo it. He was a little hazy about how he got home. He had a vague memory of hailing a cab. But it was Ilsa who had given the driver directions. He remembered being surprised that she knew where he lived, but decided he must have told her during the course of the long evening.

He rolled off the couch and stood up. "Ohh." He headed for the bathroom and ran the cold water full-force. Grabbing a washcloth, he soaked it under the spigot and pressed it to his forehead. That woman sure had a head for liquor. She had matched his beers—two for one. With his free hand, he fumbled through the medicine cabinet, looking for aspirin. No luck. He must go to the store today and stock up. He staggered back to the couch and lay down again. A loud banging on the apartment door brought him upright. Quickly pulling his trousers on over his long johns, he went to the door. "Who is it?"

"Super. Open up."

He finished fastening his belt and opened the door.

*"Činže."* (*"Rent."*) The surly man blurted the word.

"But surely my cousins . . ."

61

*"Pro Brezen, ne Duben."* (*"For March, not April."*)

The man was probably within his rights—although it was only March 31! "Just a minute." Fenimore went to the coffee table where he had dropped his wallet the night before. The super followed close behind. Fenimore skimmed through his foreign currency. "How much?"

"Four thousand korunas." (*"Two hundred dollars."*)

Fenimore counted out the bills and handed them over. The super pocketed them with a satisfied smirk. Tucking a much thinner wallet into his back pocket, Fenimore made a mental note to stop at American Express before going shopping. When the door closed, Fenimore was fully awake. The super's visit had had the effect of a cold shower. But his head still hurt. He went back to the bathroom to check once more for aspirin, or an aspirin substitute. As he rummaged through the medicine cabinet, his eye fell on a bottle of nitroglycerin tablets. He was reminded of Vlasta's cardiac condition. Sure enough—checking the patient's name on the label, he read, VLASTA BOROVY. He opened the bottle. Three-quarters full. He rummaged further and found two other cardiac medicines. Because of the nature of his departure, Vlasta had left all his medicines behind.

This time Fenimore took a real cold shower. Throughout the shower he berated himself. What the hell did he think he was doing? Going out on the town with some blonde when he should have been looking for his cousins! But he had thought the blonde might provide him with clues, he reminded himself. *Be honest, Fenimore, you stopped looking for clues after the first beer.* As he dressed, he caught sight of a shopping bag on the chair near the door. Puppets! Was he crazy? Buying toys when his cousins were in mortal danger!

He went to the computer and booted up, taking brief satisfaction in the fact that two days ago, he didn't know how to do that. When the e-mail screen appeared, he typed Jen's address and a message: (His messages sounded like telegrams, because he wanted to limit his typing as much as possible.)

Find shoebox in top of hall closet with letters from my cousin, Anna. Send them by fastest means possible. Cost no object!
Love, F

In those letters, Anna had described her husband's condition. They were the reason Fenimore had suggested she bring Vlasta to Philadelphia for an evaluation. He wanted to go over her letters now, review Vlasta's case, and make sure Fenimore had all the right medications with him when he found Vlasta (*if* he found Vlasta). He shut down the computer and prepared to go into town. The phone rang. Forgetting about possible wiretaps, he answered it.

"Hi!" Ilsa said. "I have two tickets for the theater tonight. Would you care to join me?"

*Theater! Another time-waster,* was his first reaction. Then he reconsidered. He still had questions for Ilsa. And, so far, she was his only contact. It was up to him to stay sober and keep his mind on his job. "Sounds great."

"Good. Meet me at . . ." She gave the address. "The program begins at eight o'clock."

"I'll be there." He hung up. *How am I going to sit through a play all in Czech?* he wondered. Another thought struck him: How had Ilsa known his phone number? He didn't remember giving it to her. *Idiot! She is a great friend of Anna's. Of course she would know her phone number.* That also explained how she knew his address. Some detective he was. Maybe he should call in the police after all.

The phone rang again. It must be Ilsa. He had instructed his friends at home to contact him only by e-mail. No one else knew he was here. Reluctantly, he raised the receiver.

"What are you doing today?" Her tone was proprietary.

"Except for getting some cash and food supplies, I haven't decided."

"I've been thinking. For your safety, I think you should play the tourist role to the hilt."

"Oh?"

"Yes. People may be watching the apartment—and you. You should act like a typical American tourist."

"Please—not that!"

She laughed. "You know what I mean."

"Okay. What should I do?"

"Visit all the usual sites. The castle, the cathedral, the Astronomical Clock, and—" She paused. "—I will be your tour guide."

It was Fenimore's turn to laugh.

"What is so funny?"

"What about your medieval manuscripts?"

"They can wait. This is just a—as you say in America—coffee break."

"Mead break."

Her laugh warmed him. "Where should we meet?"

They settled on a time and a place.

# CHAPTER 13

Mrs. Doyle was frying eggs in the doctor's kitchen. The town house on Spruce Street that served as Fenimore's office and home had recently taken on the aura of a daycare center or youth hostel. And Mrs. Doyle had exchanged her customary role of nurse/office manager for cook/baby-sitter. The waiting room had become a recreation room. And the doctor's bedroom had been transformed into Mrs. Doyle's temporary boudoir. Marie and Jiri had taken over the guest room. And Horatio had traded his usual role of office assistant for second-string baby-sitter and stand-up comic. Since he was on spring break, he dropped by every afternoon (he never got up until *after* noon) to take care of Marie, for which Mrs. Doyle was very grateful. It gave her time to do the shopping and other errands. Every evening after the bookstore closed, Jennifer stopped by to check on them. She usually brought some delicious dessert such as cheesecake or chocolate brownies.

"Look!" Marie burst into the kitchen, holding Sal against her chest.

Mrs. Doyle looked. The cat's furry, yellow face peered out from a frilly dolly's bonnet. "Oh, my goodness."

"Doesn't she look pretty?" Marie planted a big kiss on top of the cat's head. In the process, she must have loosened her grip, because Sal leapt to the floor and vanished.

"Shit!" said Marie.

Mrs. Doyle looked aghast.

"Rat says that all the time. Ohhh," she moaned, "now she'll go hide and I'll never find her. Here puss, puss!"

Mrs. Doyle made a note to speak to Horatio. With that one exception, Marie's English had improved immensely since she had arrived. "She'll turn up," the nurse soothed, secretly glad the poor animal had escaped. Seeing Sal in a dolly cap was akin to witnessing child abuse. "Now, come eat your breakfast." She placed the fried egg on a plate, between two neat triangles of toast, and poured a glass of orange juice.

Marie sat down and began to eat with gusto. "Where are we going today?" she asked through a mouth full of egg and toast. Mrs. Doyle frowned. Her instinct was to tell the child not to talk with her mouth full, but she wasn't sure if it was proper for her to correct her little guest's manners. She let it pass. "I haven't decided." Mrs. Doyle's feet tended to bunions and they were still recovering from yesterday's trip to the park. "Maybe we'll just stay home today and do jigsaw puzzles."

Marie looked out the window. "Puzzles are for rainy days," she said matter-of-factly.

Following her gaze, Mrs. Doyle noted the bright sunlight filtering into the alley next to the doctor's house.

The doorbell rang.

Marie started to jump up, but Mrs. Doyle stopped her. "Finish your breakfast," she ordered, and went to answer it.

Horatio was slouched against the doorjamb, clad in his usual coordinated outfit—black leather jacket, black jeans, black sneakers. His black boom box was tucked under one arm.

"You're up early," Mrs. Doyle said.

He slid into the vestibule. "Marie here?"

"Now, where else would she be?" Mrs. Doyle blocked his entrance to the hallway. "I want to speak to you," she said in a stage whisper.

"Huh?"

"You watch your language around that young lady."

"What . . . ?"

"This morning, when Sal jumped out of her arms, she said, 'Shit.' "

Horatio clapped a hand over his mouth, feigning shock.

"It's bad enough when *you* say it, but when it comes out of a little girl's mouth . . . And what will her parents think, if we send her home spouting street talk?"

"Hey, man, can I help it if she's a parrot?"

"You can help by watching your mouth."

"All right, already. Can I go now?"

Mrs. Doyle stepped aside.

"Hi, Rat!" Marie greeted him with a big smile.

"I brought you something." He tossed a small, red object at her. She caught it.

"Way to go!" He was impressed.

"What is it?" Marie turned the object over in her hand.

"Ain't you ever seen one?" He took it from her and began to demonstrate yo-yo technique. He made it "rock," he made it "loop," he swung it up and out and around his head, pulled it down, and made it "sleep."

Marie's eyes were wide. "Teach me."

"Now, just a minute." Mrs. Doyle did her best to maintain discipline in her day care center. "No yo-yoing until you've finished your breakfast."

Marie gobbled down the remains of her toast and egg, her eyes fixed on Horatio as he performed "Rock the Baby" and "Over the Falls" with great skill.

"Before you came, we were trying to decide what to do today. Do you have any ideas?" Mrs. Doyle began putting the breakfast dishes in the dishwasher.

The boy let his yo-yo dangle. "How 'bout the Franklin Institute?"

"That's an idea."

"What's an in-sti-tute?" asked Marie.

"Uh . . ." Horatio scratched his head.

"In this case it's like a museum," said the nurse. "A science museum."

Marie wrinkled her nose.

"There's the 'Please Touch' Museum," offered Horatio.

"What about the Poe House?" Jennifer appeared in the kitchen doorway. She had her own key.

They looked at her skeptically.

"What's the Poe House?" asked Horatio.

"Edgar Allan Poe was one of our first mystery writers and he lived on Spring Garden Street." Jennifer disappeared into the combination living/dining room, where a huge bookcase dominated one wall. She came back with a small black volume in her hand. Sitting down, she flipped it open. " 'The Tell-Tale Heart,' 'The Pit and the Pendulum,' 'The Black Cat' . . ." she read from the table of contents. "Which one shall I read?"

" 'The Black Cat' " cried Marie.

Horatio shrugged.

Mrs. Doyle continued putting the kitchen in order, and wondered why Jennifer had come by so early.

"For the most wild yet most homely narrative which I am about to pen, I neither expect nor solicit belief. . . ." Jennifer paused. "Is Sal around?"

"No," Marie said, with a sorrowful expression.

"Good," said Jennifer. "I don't think she'd approve of this story." She continued to read.

While the others got ready to go to the Poe House, Jennifer stood on a chair and pulled the shoebox from the top of the hall closet. She had it under her arm and the chair replaced by the time the little group began to congregate in the hall.

"What's that?" asked the ever-observant Horatio.

"Some letters Dr. Fenimore asked me to mail to him."

"Letters? What letters?" Mrs. Doyle was not to be caught napping.

"From his cousins. He . . ." She stopped as Marie came running down the hall.

"All set?" Jennifer asked.

They nodded.

"Unfortunately, I can't come with you. I have an important errand to run."

They looked disappointed.

"Give my love to 'The Raven,' " she called as they trooped out the front door. Jennifer had offered to give them a lift, but Mrs. Doyle had promised to take Marie on the bus.

As soon as they were gone, Jennifer drew a sheet of paper from Mrs. Doyle's desk and wrote a brief note. She anchored it with the sugar bowl. When the door closed behind her, Sal crept out from under the radiator. Listening to the silence of the empty house, she found a spot of sun and stretched luxuriantly.

It would be weeks before Fenimore found the gray and dusty dolly cap under the radiator and wondered how it got there.

# CHAPTER 14

Because things were cheaper in the Czech Republic than in the United States, Fenimore discovered that he had enough money left over after paying the rent to buy his necessities: milk, eggs, coffee, sugar, bread, and aspirin. The little grocery store down the street where he had gone before had been able to supply all his needs— even a bottle of wine. Such a thing was unheard of in Philadelphia. There had been only one embarrassing moment. When he had asked for eggs (*"vejce"*), the lady behind the counter had looked puzzled, then smiled and brought him a wooden spoon (*"vařečka"*). Fenimore shook his head and clucked like a chicken. With a laugh, the woman had produced the eggs. After that everything had gone smoothly.

He had agreed to meet Ilsa at the coffee shop where they had met the previous day. "A 'coffee break' should begin with coffee," she had told him.

It was a dull, overcast day and the coffeehouse was darker than he had remembered it. The only bright thing was Ilsa's head bending over something at a table in the back. As he came near he saw she was looking at a street map of Prague. He took the seat opposite.

She glanced up with a smile. "I'm planning our day."

Fenimore felt a flutter of anticipation. *Concentrate, you ass,* he admonished himself. *Remember your mission.* A waiter came for his order. "Espresso," Fenimore said.

"You are becoming a native." Ilsa nodded her approval.

He didn't confess to his hangover. "What have you planned?"

"We will begin with the Astronomical Clock in Old Town Square. Cross the bridge . . ." (When you say "the bridge" in Prague, everyone assumes you mean the Charles Bridge, even though there are many bridges over the Vlatava.) She traced their route with her finger on the map. "We'll work our way up the hill to Prague Castle and the Cathedral of St. Vitus. Stroll through Golden Alley. On the way back, we will visit the Strahov Library and I will show you my manuscripts. Dinner at a Czech restaurant. The theater. And afterwards, an aperitif at Café Slávia." She smiled, inordinately pleased with herself.

*And after that?* thought Fenimore, and instantly reproved himself. He swallowed his espresso in two gulps. "Let's go!" He stood up.

She folded the map and stuffed it into her huge tote bag. Fenimore paid the bill. Plenty of time to ask questions as they walked, he told himself. A whole day and evening lay before them. As they left the coffeehouse, the sun burst from behind a cloud as if conferring a blessing on them.

While they waited for the light to change at Vaclavske Namesti, two scruffy youths brushed past them, almost knocking them off the curb. Ilsa dropped her tote bag and the contents spilled out on the sidewalk.

"*Pozor!*" shouted Ilsa. (*"Look out!"*)

Ignoring her, they mounted their motorcycles parked nearby, and roared off.

Fenimore helped pick up her things. Among them was the crumpled fortune-cookie slip, from dinner the night before. He put it in his pocket, intending to throw it in the first trash can.

"Thugs!" she said indignantly. "Dregs of the Communist era."

A chill shot through Fenimore. Those youths fit Marie's description of the kidnappers. "Are there many like that?" he asked.

71

"Too many. Always looking for trouble. If you pay them, they will do anything for you. No matter how dirty."

"Kidnap?"

She paused in her stride.

"The thugs who took Anna and Vlasta looked like that, and they came on motorcycles."

"They kidnapped them on motorcycles?" She looked incredulous.

Fenimore had to admit it would be difficult. "Maybe they arrived at the apartment on motorcycles, then handed them over to someone in a waiting car when they got outside."

"That sounds more logical," said Ilsa. "Oh, poor Anna. . . ."

They were standing in the middle of the sidewalk, oblivious to the pedestrians trying to make their way around them.

"I'm sorry," Ilsa said. "I wish I could be of more help."

They began walking again.

"What would Anna and Vlasta have that someone else would want?" Fenimore said, almost to himself.

"Not money." Ilsa shook her head. "Believe me, the salaries of professors in Prague are pitiful." She smiled ruefully.

Fenimore racked his brain for some other reason. Jewelry? Unlikely. His mother was the eldest sister and she had inherited most of the valuable family pieces. Their value was largely sentimental anyway. And, if jewelry was the motive, why not just steal it, and not go to the trouble of heisting its owners! . . . What else? The only other possessions his cousins seemed to have in abundance were books. But who ever heard of kidnapping someone for their books! One particular rare book? Again, why not just steal the book?

Fenimore stopped in his tracks. Books begin as manuscripts. Could that manuscript on the history of Prague's architecture contain some valuable information? "Knowledge," he said aloud.

Ilsa stopped in midstride.

"Sometimes people are kidnapped for their knowledge," he told her. "They know something that someone else wants to find out."

"Such as?"

"I don't know. Some secret. The location of something valuable. . . . A treasure?" Fenimore thought of one of his earlier adventures.

"Fairy tales," muttered Ilsa.

"What about a code? Sometimes people need to break a code."

"In wartime, not peacetime." Ilsa squelched that idea.

"I know," he said angrily. "I'm clutching at straws."

"What?"

"Straws—it's an expression meaning . . . I'm so desperate I'm talking nonsense."

"Yes." She smiled. "I'm afraid you are."

He thought of Vlasta's medicine. Time was of the essence. Without his nitros and the longer-acting drugs, Vlasta could suffer severe chest pain—even a heart attack. It was so frustrating playing the tourist when time was short and so much was at stake. He only half-watched the quaint figures of the Apostles emerge through the little door above the Astronomical Clock.

The sun had grown warm. They were washing down sausage rolls with beer, when Fenimore raised the subject of the thugs again. "Where do those toughs hang out?" he asked unexpectedly.

Ilsa squinted at him over her foaming mug. "Some sleazy bars in New Town." She shrugged. "Why?"

"I want to go there."

Her eyes widened. "You can't do that."

"Why not? I'm not as feeble as I look. I'm trained in karate," he challenged her.

She shook her head. "You don't know them. They'd make mincemeat of you. And how would you know if they're the right thugs?"

"It's my only lead, Ilsa. And time is running out." He told her about finding Vlasta's medicine, and his heart condition.

"But they're just hirelings. They won't be able to tell you anything."

"They can tell me who hired them."

Ilsa sipped her beer in silence. When she had drained her mug, she said. "Very well. But they don't gather until late evening. We'll go after the theater. Instead of aperitifs at Café Slavia, we'll have cheap malt at Café Dábel." She grimaced. *Dábel* meant "devil."

•    •    •

The high point of Ilsa's tour for Fenimore was the St. Wenceslas Chapel. Housed in St. Vitus Cathedral, it was a fitting shrine for the Czech's most venerated saint. According to Fenimore's guidebook, the saint's body was brought to this site in 935 A.D. But worship of him didn't reach its peak until the 1300s—during the reign of Charles IV. The emperor hired his best architect and sculptor, Peter Parler, to design the chapel and the tomb.

An iron grille prevented them from entering the sacred space, but nothing stopped them from gazing through the bars. Frescoes enhanced the altar and the vaulted ceiling was decorated with gold and silver stars and an elaborate chandelier. The walls were inlaid with polished gemstones—opals, rubies, and lapis lazuli. At the back, to the right of the tomb, was a golden door.

"Behind that door lie the crown jewels," Ilsa whispered with reverence. "See the locks?"

Fenimore knew about the crown jewels. They consisted of a sword, an orb, a scepter, and a crown of incalculable worth. The crown had a special religious significance, too. Imbedded in one of its points was a thorn supposed to have come from Christ's crown of thorns. Fenimore had learned all this from his mother. But the thing he remembered best was the curse. The emperor Charles IV had placed a curse on the crown: If someone wore it who had no legitimate right to it, he would die a swift and unnatural death. This legend had proved uncannily true during the German occupation of World War Two. Reinhard Heydrich, former SS general and vicious Reichsprotektor of Prague, had placed the crown on his head and paraded it in triumph before his children. A few weeks later, while driving to his headquarters, he had been ambushed and assassinated by members of the Czech resistance. Whenever Fenimore's mother told this story, her eyes filled with tears. Not for Reinhard's murder, but for the Germans' subsequent act of retaliation: They destroyed an entire Czech town—Lidice—and executed many of its inhabitants. They also murdered many members of the

Czech resistance. Fenimore felt cold, and not from the chill of the cathedral.

"There are seven locks and seven keys to that door," Ilsa continued. "For security's sake, each key is in the custody of a different dignitary: the president, the archbishop, the lord mayor . . . The jewels are displayed only on state occasions. The last time they were on view was at the Proclamation of the Czech Republic in 1993."

As they passed from the dimly lit cathedral into the brighter square, Fenimore wondered when the crown jewels would next be displayed.

He didn't have to wonder long. Propped on an easel near the cathedral door was a yellow poster, announcing in thick, black type,

The Canonization of St. Agnes
April 3rd
1:00 P.M.
*(Crown Jewels to be displayed)*

April 3. And today was the second! Should they come? The crowds would be terrific. He pointed out the sign to Ilsa. Her reaction was strange. She grew pale. Fenimore took her arm. It was trembling. "What's wrong?"

She shook her head. "It was so cold in there. Let's walk. I just remembered, I have to make a phone call." She led him at a brisk pace across the cobblestone plaza to a gift shop. "Go buy yourself some trinkets," she told him. "I won't be long." She headed for a phone booth nearby.

# CHAPTER 15

They were running late. Ilsa's phone call had gone on for some time. She had seemed to be chewing someone out vigorously—and at length. Then, Fenimore had lingered over her medieval manuscripts at the Strahov Library. As a result there was no time for a leisurely Czech dinner (*surprise! surprise!*). Instead, they grabbed sandwiches at a street stall and rushed to the theater. The heading on the marquee surprised Fenimore: PRAGUE PUPPET THEATER: "CHARLES IV," od REDIKA.

"Redik, Redik . . . Why is that name familiar?" mumbled Fenimore.

"Because you spoke to him yesterday at the University," Ilsa said.

Was that only yesterday? It seemed like years ago.

"I hope you don't mind not going to a traditional play," Ilsa said. "But you were so enchanted by those puppets last night, I thought . . ."

"Absolutely! I'd love to see a puppet show. Is Redik the chief puppeteer?"

She nodded. "The best puppet master in Prague. It is his hobby. Tonight's production is an old Czech legend he has re-created for marionettes, starring Charles IV."

"Fabulous. Lead on."

They entered the crowded lobby. The first thing Fenimore noticed was the absence of children.

"Oh, in Prague many puppet shows are not for children. Some of the action is quite risqué."

"Hmm." The evening was looking up.

Ilsa had purchased excellent seats in the third row from which it was possible to see the smallest detail of the puppets' painted faces and every stitch of their exquisite costumes. As the curtain rose, "the Emperor" was on his throne, dressed in a velvet cloak of midnight-blue, trimmed with creamy ermine. On his head he wore the Czech crown. The pasteboard jewels glittered and sparkled every time he turned his head. His face was not stern, but benign. All the facsimiles of Charles IV, in sculpture and paintings throughout the city, portrayed him as kindly, Fenimore realized. The eyes were the most striking feature of the puppets' faces. They were larger in proportion to the rest of their features—almost bulbous—like in the sculptured figures that decorate churches and cathedrals. In both cases, the eyes were emphasized, to make them more visible from a distance, whether on a stage or embedded high in a church wall. Later, Ilsa told him that many puppet carvers were employed during the day as church sculptors, and puppet carving was a hobby, reserved for the evening hours. Most of the marionettes they would see tonight were over a hundred years old.

As the Emperor sat on his throne, the Town Crier was brought before him bearing an important message: "There is no work in the land. The people have no money. They are roaming the countryside, begging for food. And conditions are worsening. People are starving. They have no bread for their families."

Charles IV became distraught. He bent his head, placing his wooden face in his wooden hands. From offstage, the plaintive music of a lute could be heard. Suddenly the Emperor raised his head. He had an idea. He stepped down from his throne and called for a conference with his Chief Ministers. They appeared in black robes, some with beards, all with large, staring eyes. Bending their heads together, they nodded wisely. Finally Charles emerged from the group and spoke to the Crier: "Take this message back to my people," he said. "Tell them I want to build a great wall beside the river Vlatava, and I need many workmen. They should come to the Castle tomorrow at dawn. If they work well, they will receive enough bread to feed their families."

The Crier rubbed his hands together and took off, ringing his bell. "Hear ye! Hear ye!" he chanted as the curtain fell.

When the lights came up, Fenimore also rubbed his hands together, pleased with himself. He had understood every word. The puppets' language was simple. He was enjoying the puppet show more than he would have enjoyed a traditional play, he told Ilsa.

She seemed pleased. Rising, she led him out of the row.

Fenimore followed. "Where are we going?" He had expected to go to the lobby for refreshments, but Ilsa was heading down the aisle, toward the stage. She opened a door at one side of the stage. There was the smell of sweat, greasepaint, and tobacco. She led him to another door on which was stenciled REDIK in small black letters. Such small letters for the star of the show?

Ilsa's hand was poised to knock, when a voice on the other side thundered, "I am the Emperor—master of all!"

Ilsa looked at Fenimore warily, to see if he understood. Fenimore made a pretense of bewilderment.

"I am *your* master!" the voice bellowed, with such force that Fenimore involuntarily stepped back from the door.

Ilsa frowned. "Rehearsing," she whispered apologetically. She waited a moment before knocking.

"Come in."

When they entered, Fenimore didn't recognize the professor at first.

Redik was stretched out on a chaise lounge, wearing a silk bathrobe, smoking a cigarette. "Ilsa!" He half rose. "I didn't expect . . ."

"Don't get up." She waved him back.

A slim young woman in an abbreviated outfit—short shorts, a skintight tank top, and sandals—emerged from behind a screen. "I'll be backstage, Jan," she murmured, and headed for the door.

Ilsa's gaze followed her out and there was an awkward pause. Redik turned to Fenimore. "Now you see me in my other persona." He laughed. "Cigarette?"

"No, thanks."

"Ah, that's right. The Americans have repudiated the cigarette. More power to you." He continued smoking.

Redik seemed much more at home in his dressing room than in his office at the University.

"Your puppets are marvelous," said Fenimore.

"You like them?"

"Tremendously."

"Have you made any progress with finding your relatives?"

Fenimore glanced at Ilsa. "No," he said.

"Will you have a glass of wine? Or is that outlawed in America, too?"

"You make me feel like a Puritan. I'd love a glass of wine. A recent study has revealed that red wine—in moderation—is good for the heart."

Ilsa disappeared behind the screen and they heard the clink of glasses.

"Where are your puppets?" Fenimore looked around the sparsely furnished room. Unlike most dressing rooms, this one lacked the usual clutter of makeup or costumes. The puppeteer needs neither thought Fenimore. No one expects him to dress up. He remains hidden from the audience until the very end, when he answers his curtain call. He could appear in workclothes—a pair of overalls and a sweatshirt.

"They are hung on special hooks in a cupboard behind the stage. They are old and fragile. The less they are moved, except during a performance, the better."

Ilsa appeared with only two glasses of wine.

"Wine may be good for the heart, but not for the mind," Redik explained. "I need all my wits during a performance. Afterward I will drink to my heart's content—to all our hearts,' " he added.

"Yes, your wits have been slipping lately," Ilsa muttered, unexpectedly.

Redik glanced at her sharply.

Fenimore wondered if Redik had been the recipient of Ilsa's angry phone call. He had detected a certain animosity between the two since they had entered the dressing room. "How did you get into this puppet thing?" he asked Redik.

"Since a boy, I have always loved puppets. The art of puppetry has a long and proud Czech history—stretching back to the Middle Ages. . . . In Bohemia many families had their own puppets and performed shows not just for children but whole villages. They were precious possessions—as valuable as the family silver. During World War Two they hid them in their cellar walls and chimneys."

There was a power in this man—a magnetic pull—that Fenimore had been unaware of before. It affected Ilsa, too, he noticed. Despite her former irritation, her gaze was fixed on him now, like a puppet to a string.

"Under the Hapsburgs," Redik continued, "the only theater in which the Czechs were allowed to speak their native language was the puppet theater. The official language was German. The authorities mistakenly thought puppet shows were too low to matter. They were wrong. The shows were full of buffoons making fun of the nobility, and they sowed the seeds for the later revolution."

"The Nazis weren't so stupid," put in Ilsa. "They stamped out puppet shows from the beginning."

"True, and so did the Communists," said Redik. "You see, Doctor, the Czechs are always being oppressed by someone. We are not allowed to express our thoughts and feelings. We must go underground and let the puppets do it for us."

"But surely now—"

"In 1989," Ilsa broke in, "on the eve of the Velvet Revolution, Redik and other puppeteers took to the streets mocking the Communist regime with their puppets."

"But today there is no reason to use puppets for political purposes," Fenimore reminded them. "You are free, and—"

"You Americans have a puppet of your own," Redik changed the subject. "The one Walter Disney made famous?"

"Oh, you mean Pinocchio?"

"Yes, the boy with the long nose," said Ilsa. "It grew a little more every time he told a lie."

"But, that story originated in Italy—" A bell interrupted Fenimore.

Redik sat up and crushed out his cigarette. It was time to go. Ilsa finished her wine. Fenimore followed suit. They thanked him and hurried back to their seats. Before the curtain rose, Fenimore asked, "Who was the young woman in the dressing room when we arrived?"

"Ema." Ilsa frowned. "An intern from the School of the Arts. She is studying under Redik and helps with the performances."

Act Two opened with Charles IV on his balcony. A group of peasants was gathered beneath him, cheering. The Emperor made sweeping gestures and spoke with eloquence. He told them The Wall was coming along well. People were eating again. He was pleased. He would never allow his people to go hungry again. From now on, the wall would be called "The Bread Wall."

Cheers. One man's voice rose above the others. *"Děkuji,"* he cried. (*"Thank you."*)

The Emperor bowed. As he did so, his crown fell off.

There was a gasp from the real audience as well as the crowd of puppets.

The man who had spoken caught the crown. (No mean feat for a puppet!)

"That's Kasparek," Ilsa whispered. "The clown."

Twisting and turning the circle of jewels, Kasparek stared at it. The Emperor reached down, expecting the man to hand it back to him. Instead, he deliberately placed it on his own head.

Again the audience gasped.

The man pranced around the stage, doing a two-step and crowing. "I am the Emperor. I am master over you." He waved at the crowd. After circling the stage, he pointed upward—at the Emperor: "I am *your* master!" He laughed.

The crowd made a lunge for him as the curtain fell.

"When is the risqué part?" asked Fenimore.

"Now," said Ilsa, "this is a little something extra—a soupçon, if you will. It has nothing to do with the main story."

The curtain rose again, revealing two puppets—a peasant man and woman. The woman shouted something at the man. The man pulled out a stick and began beating her with it. She ran across the stage. There was a haystack on the other side. She disappeared behind it. The man followed. When they came out, they were both naked. The man knocked her down and they fornicated then and there. The puppeteer pulled their strings in perfect unison. They were still at it when the curtain fell. The audience roared.

"A porno Punch and Judy," said Fenimore. He was surprised to see Ilsa blush.

In the lobby, as they sipped their orange drinks, Fenimore grew restless. Glancing out the window, he saw the tram lights glowing in the dark. The bar where Ilsa had promised to take him would be filling up. He was itching to get going.

Act Three. The curtain rose on the Emperor sitting alone in his tower. Bare-headed and clad in a simple white robe, he looked weak—vulnerable. He was grieving for his people. Without his crown, he said, he felt impotent, unable to take care of his kingdom. The Ministers organized a search party to look for the thief. Soldier puppets in gleaming armor roamed the hills and dales. A solemn drumbeat accompanied their search, the thief was nowhere to be found.

Darkness fell. Suddenly, the window in a cabin at the back of the stage, which had gone unnoticed before, lit up. Inside, the silhouette of the thief could be seen, still dancing, still wearing the crown in the yellow square of light. Slowly the soldiers approached, surrounding the cabin. The head officer pounded on the door. *"Otevřid!"* he cried. (*"Open!"*) The light in the window went out. All was dark and silent on the stage, for what seemed to Fenimore to be a very long time. But the audience remained perfectly still. When the scream came, Fenimore almost jumped out of his seat.

During this intermission, Fenimore challenged Ilsa. "There's something wrong with the plot," he said. "Shouldn't Kasparek be the good guy? He always was, in the tales my mother told me."

Ilsa cocked an eyebrow at him. "In the old days that was true." She drained her glass and set it down. "Times change."

The next scene was the Castle. Charles IV appeared in full regalia, wearing his crown. He was hosting a ball. It was a lavish celebration. The castle hall was filled with people dining, drinking, and dancing. The Emperor moved through the crowd, nodding to the people, greeting them with all the grandeur and geniality of a good and great ruler. The lute player sat at the base of the stairwell, playing for all he was worth. The people danced on and on. At last, the Emperor stepped forward and made a deep bow to the real audience. But this time he held on to his crown with one hand.

The audience went wild. Fenimore detected all the fervor of a recently oppressed people. To them the crown represented the restoration of their country and all that it stood for.

But Fenimore felt vaguely dissatisfied with the play. Something was lacking. Shouldn't there have been more emphasis on freedom—and independence?

The curtain closed, the clapping and cheering died down. But no one made a move to leave. The curtains parted and Redik stepped out. In a pair of baggy jeans and an oversized sweatshirt he seemed smaller than ever. Removing his glasses, he bowed slightly. Once again, the audience erupted. Fenimore glanced at Ilsa. Her eyes were fixed on the puppet master, but her expression was inscrutable.

# CHAPTER 16

The visit to the Poe House was a great success. With one exception. While they were waiting in line for tickets, Horatio accidentally hit the woman in front of him with his yo-yo. Not hard. He was just practicing a new trick called "Slurp the Spaghetti" and one of the slurps glanced off the back of the woman's calf. She let out a yelp, turned and glared at him.

"Sorry," he muttered.

"Put that thing away," ordered Mrs. Doyle.

An earnest young woman guided them through each of the rooms in the creaky old house. Mrs. Doyle suspected the ghost of Poe was lurking in every closet. In one room there was a desk by a window, with an ink well and an old quill pen resting on it. The guide told them the great author had looked out that very window when he had penned "The Pit and the Pendulum."

Now, how could she possibly know that? Mrs. Doyle wondered.

At the end of the tour they watched a video of Basil Rathbone reading "The Tell-Tale Heart." Its awful beats echoed in their heads long after the film was over. Mrs. Doyle worried that Marie would have nightmares.

But the high point of their visit was the Raven, perched on a pedestal in the backyard, its black wings spread. Here, the guide recited the first three stanzas of the poem by the same name with emotion. Mrs. Doyle shivered at each "Nevermore." But the somber refrain had little effect on her two companions. Horatio yawned repeatedly. Marie hunted for dandelions in the spring grass.

When the tour was over, Horatio and Marie announced they were hungry. Mrs. Doyle remembered a diner on Spring Garden Street, called Silk City. As they walked, Marie repeated the name, "Silk City, Silk City." She liked the way the foreign words slid off her tongue. She also liked the diner. Diners were a novelty to Marie. A strictly American invention. And, unlike McDonald's, they had not yet crossed the Atlantic. She loved the gleaming coffeemaker behind the counter, the cakes and pies displayed under their plastic covers, the cozy booths, and especially the chance to play her favorite songs by dropping a coin in the slot of the jukebox at her elbow. There was something very satisfying about putting a coin in a slot and getting something you wanted in return. Maybe *that* was at the root of gambling, the reason Atlantic City was such a success, thought Mrs. Doyle.

She had a moment of nostalgia, remembering the old Automat on Market Street and what a kick she had gotten from dropping her nickels in the slot and getting a piece of moist apple pie, a pot of steaming baked beans, or a dish of creamy rice pudding. Her memories were interrupted by a tug on her sleeve. Marie was calling her attention to the waitress who stood patiently by, waiting for her order.

"Apple pie, baked beans, and rice pudding," Mrs. Doyle said.

The waitress raised an eyebrow. "All at once?"

"No," Mrs. Doyle said briskly. "One after the other."

The woman jotted down the order and took off.

Horatio and Marie had a battle over which songs to play. He wanted rock 'n' roll; she wanted country music.

"How can you stand that sh—" He caught himself in time. ". . . corny stuff?"

"What's 'corny'?" Marie asked.

Mrs. Doyle eagerly awaited Horatio's reply.

"Old-timey. Hayseed. Hicksville."

Looking even more mystified, Marie said simply, "I like the tunes."

They listened to country music.

It was almost four o'clock when they got back to the house. They had taken two buses and one of them was long in coming. The youngsters went directly into the waiting room–turned–rec room where Horatio could demonstrate his latest yo-yo tricks without injuring anyone. Mrs. Doyle climbed the stairs to her bedroom "to take a load off my feet." It was almost seven when hunger pangs woke her and she went downstairs to prepare supper.

The first thing she saw was Jennifer's note on the kitchen table. She shoved the sugar bowl aside and read:

*Dear Friends,*

*By the time you read this I will be on my way to Prague. The doctor said he wanted those letters delivered as fast as possible and I was able to book a flight. You seemed to be getting along so well, there was no reason for me to stick around. I'll be back next week. Take care.*

*Jen*

"*Humph*. She could have *told* us," muttered Mrs. Doyle. "I wonder if she told *him*? What a surprise. . . ." The romantic in the nurse stirred as she imagined their meeting. Mrs. Doyle had been in love once. She thought of her husband, Ed, fondly. They had had their share of surprises. She remembered the time—

"What's for dinner?" Horatio stood in the doorway.

Ever since Marie had arrived, he seemed to have become a full-time boarder.

"Have you called your mother?"

"She knows I'm here," he said nonchalantly.

Mrs. Doyle wasn't too surprised by Horatio's willingness to spend time with Marie. He had brothers and sisters, but they were all older.

He had never experienced the heady sensation of having a younger sibling who looked up to him and whom he could order around. It had its appeal.

"Can we have ice cream?" Marie had become addicted to that Philadelphia specialty.

"Shoo!" Mrs. Doyle sent them both out of the kitchen and told them to set the table. Here she was, supposed to be on vacation, and she was working harder than ever. As she molded the hamburgers, she hummed a few bars of "When Irish Eyes Are Smiling."

# CHAPTER 17

Nové Město, or "New Town," did not look very new by American standards. In fact, it was built in the late seventeenth century, right around the time William Penn was laying out Philadelphia. There were more bars and restaurants in this section of Prague than in other parts of the city. Ilsa forged ahead, steering Fenimore from the swanky tourist watering holes to a string of shabbier, seamier bars and taverns.

Fenimore spotted the motorcycles first. Row upon row were double-parked along the curb. They gleamed purple under the glow of the neon sign—CAFE DABEL. When they were still a block away, Ilsa stopped and placed her hands around Fenimore's neck. For a moment he thought she was going to do something impulsive. Instead, she merely stripped off his tie, undid the top two buttons of his shirt, and rumpled his hair (what remained of it).

"Hey!" he objected.

"You don't want to stand out too much," she told him. She produced a compact, lipgloss, and mascara from her enormous tote bag, and began to work on her face. She coated her lips with gloss and tinted her eyelashes with silver. Removing the tortoiseshell comb that held her hair neatly in place, it fell loosely around her shoulders.

Finally, she gave her blouse a yank, baring one ample shoulder.

Fenimore stared. "Medieval scholar becomes 'lady of the night,' " he said.

"Like it?" She batted her silver lashes at him and formed her shiny lips into a sultry pout.

"Holy mackerel!"

She looked perplexed—unsure whether to be pleased or hurt.

"Sorry. That's an American expression." He grabbed her hand. "Let's go."

The noise of the café reached them when they were still a block away. Ilsa paused again. "Now, listen," she warned, "don't start talking to people and asking too many questions. We go in, drink for a while, blend in with the crowd. See what's going on. . . ."

" 'Get the lay of the land,' as we say in the States."

She nodded. "And let me start the conversations. You play the strong, silent type for one night. Could you smoke a cigarette?"

He grimaced.

"It would help your image." Once again, she burrowed into her tote bag and came up with the necessary equipment. A crumpled pack of Lucky Strikes and a book of matches.

He frowned. "Do you . . . ?"

"Once in a while," she said blandly, stowing the cigarettes and matches in his shirt pocket. "Come on."

A tidal wave of noise, smoke, and the odor of stale beer washed over them. Anxious to play his part well, Fenimore found himself thinking of Horatio—his role model. How would he act? *Stay cool. . . .*! He could hear the teenager's familiar drawl. *Don't walk—slide. Don't sit—lounge. Don't talk much—grunt.* Never *smile.*

Thuggery, the world over, was much the same.

They edged between the close-packed sweaty bodies, their eyes smarting from the smoke, their ears throbbing from the noise. Ilsa spied some people vacating a table near the bar. She pushed him into it. He leaned back languidly, letting his eyes slide over the other customers. Too John Wayne-ish. He sat up and grabbed a passing waiter, *"Dvě Plzně,"* he ordered. He slipped a cigarette from the pack and let Ilsa light it for him. Catching her eye above the flame, he saw that she approved of him. After his first inhale, he coughed, nearly spoiling it.

He asked where she had learned her knack for being a quick-change artist.

"I always wanted to be an actress," she said. "But there's not much demand for Brunnhildes who can't sing." She glanced ruefully down at her ample chest and belly.

That explained her interest in Redik, thought Fenimore. She had transferred her love of the theater to the puppet master and his hobby. She was living her dream vicariously.

As they drank and smoked—Ilsa had lit up, too—Fenimore noticed some of the scruffy youths eyeing her, despite her girth. He also noticed that he didn't like it. One especially muscular specimen leaned down from his barstool and spoke to her. She shook her head, keeping her eyes on Fenimore. The youth shrugged and returned to his beer. Most of the clientele was male—youths between the ages of sixteen and twenty-five. Although decorated with tattoos and earrings, they had none of the colorful, swashbuckling air of real pirates. There was something gray and sticky about them—like leftover oatmeal. How would he find out anything from them?

Noting his depressed expression, Ilsa reached over and pressed his hand. Soon she rose and disappeared. To the restroom, Fenimore guessed. He ordered two more beers from the bar. When he turned back to the table, Ilsa's empty chair was occupied. He wanted to tell the interloper to beat it, but the fellow was bigger than he was, and not quite sober. He decided when Ilsa came back, the situation would take care of itself.

It didn't. When Ilsa came back to the table, the man stayed put, ignoring her. Fenimore had to do something, but without causing a confrontation. He rose and gave Ilsa his chair. As she settled into it, he went to the restroom. While there, he tried to think what to do next. The restroom was not conducive to thought. It was filthy, and stank. When he returned, he was surprised to find Ilsa and the stranger talking animatedly. As Fenimore approached the table, she shot him an eye signal: *Stay away*. He turned his back and ordered a beer from the bar.

He finished the beer before turning to see how things were progressing behind him. Ilsa sat alone, staring morosely into her glass. She seemed more than a little drunk. He joined her. To his horror, she began to cry. "Take me home," she pleaded. They rose and he ushered her through the crowd, which had grown thicker since they had arrived. As they walked down the street, Ilsa leaned against him, keeping her head low.

"What's wrong?" Fenimore whispered.

"Nothing. But we may be watched," she whispered back. Not until they had passed from the purple glow of the café sign to the darkness beyond, did she move away and become herself again.

"What happened?" He was on pins and needles.

"That man knew one of the hirelings."

"What?"

"It's not that much of a coincidence," she said. "Apparently, the kidnapping story has been circulating for some time. They all know about it. The thugs responsible bragged about it at the bar for days. . . ."

"But who hired them?"

"Some syndicate. They thought your cousins were involved in drug trafficking—infringing on their territory.

"Oh my god."

"I know. Can you imagine Anna and Vlasta dealing drugs? They were kidnapped to teach them a lesson."

Fenimore paled. "Who is behind this syndicate? How can we find them?"

"He wouldn't tell me. When he found out I wasn't going to leave with him, he shut up like a clam."

"How could such a thing happen?"

"Misidentification? It happened all the time under the Communists. The wrong people getting killed. . . ."

Fenimore stood still.

"I'm sorry. I shouldn't have said that." She touched his arm contritely.

"That's all right." He squeezed her hand. "You found out a lot, and I'm very grateful." As they walked on, he wondered how he was going to deal with this new information.

# CHAPTER 18

They were on the subway when they both realized they were starved. All they had eaten since noon was a sandwich. Escapades like theirs tended to increase the appetite.

"We could go back to the Café Slavia. It stays open until three A.M.," she suggested. "Or we could go to your place," she said casually. "It's not far from here."

Suddenly the thought of being alone was unbearable. "Come back to my place," he said quickly, as if it were his idea. "I have a nice bottle of wine and I make a mean scrambled egg," he added.

She smiled. "All right."

Fenimore wrestled with the eggs while Ilsa set the table. He would have been happy to eat in the kitchen, but she had insisted on the dining room. After he showed her where things were, she set out two plates, two forks, and two wineglasses. She was lighting the candles and Fenimore was vigorously stirring the eggs, when the apartment buzzer buzzed.

"Who could that be?" Fenimore checked his watch. After midnight. He started for the door.

"Be careful," Ilsa cautioned.

*It's probably the super,* he thought, *after me for more money.* "Who is it?" he called out.

"Jen."

He looked around wildly. The wineglasses glittered in the candlelight. So did Ilsa's lipgloss. He felt his open shirt. "Just a minute." He started to button his shirt but, feeling Ilsa's eyes on him, left it, and opened the door.

"Surprise!" Jennifer handed him the shoebox full of letters and stepped inside. "You said to send these as fast as possible and cost was no object. I caught a red-eye flight and came straight from the airport." She scanned the room, her eyes pausing at the entrance to the dining room.

"I'd like you to meet Ilsa Tanaček. She's helping me find my cousins," he mumbled.

Jennifer took in the candles, the wineglasses, and Ilsa.

"Let me have your coat." Fenimore set the shoebox on the coffee table.

"No," Jennifer said quickly, "I have to get to my hotel or they won't hold the room for me."

"But . . ."

"And my cab is waiting," she lied.

"Where are you staying? I'll call you in the morning."

"The Cloister Inn. But don't bother. I'll be leaving early. I just wanted you to have the letters. I thought they might be important." She disappeared through the still-open door.

"Jen. . . ." He started after her.

Ilsa coughed.

He turned.

"I'm still hungry," she said.

Slowly, he closed the door and went back to the kitchen.

Fenimore burnt the eggs. While he was making a second batch, Ilsa opened the wine and offered him some. He refused. She poured herself a glass and took it into the living room. When the eggs were ready, they ate quickly. As soon as Ilsa departed, Fenimore tried to call Jen at her hotel. She wasn't answering her phone. Finally, to take his mind off his troubles, he attacked the shoebox full of letters.

Sifting through them, he read snatches from each year. The batch Jennifer had brought began in the early 1980s. Anna had always written to his mother in Czech. But after she died, Anna had written to his father in English. To decipher the early letters would have been too difficult, that's the reason he had not asked for them. Most of the letters were exceedingly dull. Accounts of births, deaths, illnesses, et cetera of family members Fenimore had never met. Only one caught his eye. It was longer than the rest and had been written about six months ago. He must have read it before, but without paying much attention.

*Vlasta and I continue to research our book. Today we explored St. Vitus Cathedral. We searched for signs of secret doors, passageways, and staircases. Our efforts did not go unrewarded. In the crypt, directly below the Wenceslaus Chapel, we discovered a door that opened to a narrow staircase. The staircase—in turn—led to the door of the chamber that contains the crown jewels! The first door is carefully concealed from the naked eye. A thin crack, about the width of a spiderweb strand, was the only evidence. We discovered it with the aid of a high-powered electric torch. The second door, at the top of the stairs, was locked— but with only one lock, and not a very complicated one. As we are not in the lock-picking business, we went no further.*

*But one cannot underestimate the importance of this discovery. The crown jewels can be reached without the complicated use of multiple locks and keys, which we had been led to believe were necessary. Apparently, Charles IV created his elaborate traditional ceremony purely for a show of security! I am telling you this, because I know it will be safe with you. Vlasta and I were bursting with our historic discovery but could share it with no one here for obvious reasons. It was very frustrating. Wouldn't some robber love*

*to know our secret? Unfortunately, we will be unable to
include our find in our architecture book. In this case,
national security must take precedence over intellectual
honesty. Such a pity!*

Fenimore had been reading intently. When he finished he went over to the bookcase to retrieve the manuscript. He wanted to check the plan of the cathedral to see the exact location Anna had described. He inhaled sharply. On the shelf, where the manuscript had been, was a large gap.

Who had been in the apartment since he had last looked there?

The super? He had a key and could come in any time. And Ilsa. While he was in the kitchen, could she have. . . . ? But how did she conceal such a bulky item? The image of a large blue tote bag rose before him. He closed his eyes—and cursed.

Later, when preparing for bed, Fenimore reached in his jacket pocket to remove his loose change. Among the coins was Ilsa's crumpled fortune slip. He didn't know what possessed him to open it.

*Expect a financial windfall.*

Even though his Czech was rusty, Fenimore knew the words did not say "romance with a foreigner."

# CHAPTER 19

The next morning, right after breakfast, Mrs. Doyle trudged over to Nicholson Books to see if there were any e-mail messages from Prague. Mr. Nicholson, Jennifer's father, greeted her cordially. "You know, Mrs. Doyle, I'd be glad to check those messages for you and call you if there's anything important. It would save you a trip."

"That's very kind of you. But sometimes I might have to send a quick answer."

"Well, you could dictate your answer over the phone and I could type it for you."

"Thanks. But you have enough to do, managing the store without Jennifer."

"Yes. Her departure was rather sudden."

"Someday I hope we'll have a computer of our own," Mrs. Doyle said.

"I'm sure when the doctor returns, he'll see the necessity of one."

Mrs. Doyle wasn't so sure. But she had to admit she wasn't completely without blame. She had clung to her old standard typewriter and never had encouraged the doctor to buy high-tech office equipment.

*"You have mail,"* the computer sang out. She read the message on the screen:

Dear Mrs. Doyle,
  I have arranged via the Internet for you to take Marie to the zoo tomorrow. Two tickets are reserved for you at the Gate under my name. Pick them up at 10:00 A.M.
  Sincerely,
  Dr. Fenimore

*How formal,* thought Doyle. And no word about Jennifer. She should have arrived by now. She was pondering this message so long, Mr. Nicholson asked, "Anything wrong?"

"I don't know." She moved aside to let him view the screen.

"Hmm."

"A trifle formal for the doctor, don't you think?" she said.

He nodded. "But he's just begun to use e-mail. People tend to be more formal in the beginning—until they get used to it."

"I suppose. Do you think I should pick up the tickets, then?"

"Certainly. Tomorrow's weather forecast is 'clear and sunny.' A perfect day for the zoo."

Mrs. Doyle's feet began to ache in anticipation.

# CHAPTER 20

Fenimore was up at sunrise, fretting over Jennifer. But he didn't dare call her until midmorning, knowing that she would be dead to the world after her plane flight. At ten, he could restrain himself no longer. Her "Hello?" was thick with sleep.

"I have to see you."

"Oh?" Her single, sharp utterance was not encouraging.

"I want to explain about last night."

"Don't bother. I understood perfectly."

"It wasn't what you think. . . ."

"How do you know what I think? I'm booking an evening flight back to Philadelphia."

"That's how I know what you think. Please don't go."

A long pause.

"You can't leave without seeing the city. . . ."

"I can. I am."

He tried a different tact. "There have been some disturbing developments regarding my cousins' disappearance."

"Oh?" The word had lost some of its brittleness.

"Last night, after Ilsa left, a few minutes after *you* left," he interjected, "I went through the letters you brought and found an interesting item. When I went to check the item out in my cousins' manuscript—the architecture book they're working on—the manuscript was gone!"

"Gone?"

"I think Ilsa may have taken it." There was a lengthy pause. "I'm afraid I've been a total ass," he admitted.

A longer silence ensued. Finally Jennifer said, "You always had a weakness for blondes."

"You're not a blonde."

"I was the exception."

"Was?"

She didn't answer.

"I have to get going," he said.

"Where to?"

"To find Ilsa and confront her with the theft."

"Do you think that's wise?"

"What do you mean?"

"Well, wouldn't it be better to pretend you didn't notice, and continue to see her? You might be able to find out more about your cousins."

"You're right. You see, I need you."

More silence.

"I'll pick you up at noon." Fenimore forged ahead.

"But I have jet lag. . . . I haven't even had my morning coffee. . . . I—"

"I'll call you back in ten minutes."

"No. I'll call you." She hung up.

Fenimore sweated for ten, fifteen, twenty minutes. To fill the time he checked his e-mail. Nothing.

The phone rang, jarring him. He picked it up.

"I've postponed my flight. But only until tomorrow."

"Great. I'll see you in the lobby at noon." He hung up before she could change her mind.

As Fenimore stepped out of the apartment, he saw the super edging his way down the hall. The word *slinking* came to mind. Had he been listening? He remembered Marie pointing to the wall and then to her ear. He shook his head and hurried toward the bus stop.

# CHAPTER 21

As Fenimore disembarked in the center of Prague, a poster caught his eye. The same yellow poster he had seen outside the St. Vitus Cathedral when he was with Ilsa. A reminder that the Canonization of Saint Agnes was to take place that day and the crown jewels would be on display.

The Cloister Inn was only a few blocks from the bus stop. The small lobby was empty except for a desk clerk and an elderly woman sipping free coffee offered at a table nearby. He helped himself to a cup. Prague coffee was the best he had ever tasted. He sat down to wait for Jennifer. He didn't have to wait long. Jennifer did not play games. If she was angry at Fenimore, she would tell him; she wouldn't make him pay by keeping him waiting or making him miserable in other mean little ways.

She wore a black pants suit with a turquoise silk blouse. Despite her remonstrance about jet lag, she looked surprisingly wide-awake and ready to go. "What's the plan?" she asked.

"I thought we'd start with the cathedral."

"Fine." She handed her room key to the desk clerk.

It was warm for April. Some men had removed their topcoats

and were carrying them over their arms. One woman was wearing a straw hat. The cobblestones glistened in the sun. They must have been washed by an early-morning shower. The dampness brought out the designs and patterns in the stones—circles, diamonds, zigzags—in varying shades of gray. They reminded him of the brickwork in south Jersey. How he wished they could just enjoy the day, without the burden of looking for his relatives. Then he cursed himself for being such a selfish bastard.

"Now—why the cathedral?" Jennifer asked.

He told her about the canonization ceremony and the crown jewels. "They are only shown on rare occasions. The last time they were on display was after the Velvet Revolution—in 1989. This is the chance of a lifetime."

"But what do they have to do with finding your cousins?"

"I'm not sure. . . ." He frowned. "It's just a hunch. But everywhere I've turned since I came here, I've bumped into the crown jewels." He told her about Redik and the puppet show in which Charles IV lost his crown. And about the passage in Anna's letter that described the secret entrance to the chamber where the jewels are stored. And now this opportunity to see them on display. "It just seems important for me to be there," he concluded weakly, searching her face for confirmation.

"Let's go," she said.

The Charles Bridge was even more crowded than usual. He was about to point out Bruncvik—the brave knight—to Jennifer, but decided against it. There wasn't time. The ceremony began at one o'clock and it was already twelve-fifteen. Once across the bridge, all the ways leading to the Hrad, Prague Castle, were jammed. Fenimore began to have second thoughts about his plan. Even if they could get inside the cathedral, would they be able to see the jewels? Of course, the weather didn't help. The beautiful, mild day had brought everybody out. But it was a polite crowd. No pushing or shoving. Gradually, they made their orderly way up the steep stone steps onto the grand plaza before the wrought-iron gates.

Jennifer gazed at the statues of the two giants—one wielding a club, the other a dagger—on top of the gates. "I wouldn't want to tangle with them."

Locating *The Battling Giants* in his guidebook, Fenimore declared, "They're only copies."

"They look real enough to me." As Jennifer passed through the gates, she noted the palace guards in their attractive uniforms— navy-blue, with red-and-gold trim.

"Havel ordered those festive outfits to replace the dull khaki ones the Communist guards wore," Fenimore said. The young guards maintained a rigid demeanor, until a pretty teenager waved at them. Then they had to work hard not to crack a smile.

The throng inched across the square toward the wide cathedral doorways. Many were better dressed than Fenimore and Jennifer, decked out in their best attire for the occasion. *At least I'm wearing a tie,* he thought, *and Jennifer looks good in anything.*

As they neared the entrance Jennifer whispered, "By the way, who is Saint Agnes?"

"She was Sister Agnes—a member of the convent." And Fenimore retold the story his mother had told him years ago. "She saved many refugees during World War Two—Jews and Romanies, who were Gypsies, especially children—hiding them in the wine cellar of the convent. When her work was discovered, she was captured— and killed."

Jennifer shivered.

The history of Prague was full of such dark tales, Fenimore thought. Jan Palach—the young student who, during the Prague Spring in 1968, set himself on fire to protest the Communist takeover. The members of the Czech resistance who assassinated Reinhard Heydrich—the wicked Reichsprotektor—and were destroyed in turn by the Nazis in 1942. And Jan Masaryk, son of the founder of Czech independence, who fell (or was pushed) from his bedroom window one night in 1948 and found dead in the courtyard below. Václav Havel, himself, had been imprisoned for his part in Charter 77, the human rights document created during the brief "Prague

Spring" in 1968 under Dubček. Victims, all, of vicious groups wanting to take over their native land. And these were only the ones Fenimore remembered by name. Hundreds of others had died, nameless to history.

The vast cathedral was packed with people, shoulder to shoulder. The only space was above the crowd, soaring to the vaulted ceiling. Candles flickered in their sconces, aided by electric lights, skillfully hidden in niches and recesses among the sculpture on the walls and pillars. The organ boomed the opening chords of the Czech national anthem, a signal for the throng to disperse and make room for the parade of dignitaries about to enter.

Fenimore grabbed Jennifer's hand and pulled her toward the Wenceslaus Chapel. Squeezing against the iron grille, they caught a fleeting glimpse of the crown jewels before guards forced them back to make way for the promenade. The procession was headed by the archbishop, in full regalia, followed by lesser church officials decked out in their most colorful finery. Behind them walked President Havel in a simple dark business suit. No pomp or frills for him. Fenimore's chest swelled with emotion at the sight of this unassuming man, whose courage and sacrifice had led his country to freedom. After him came the cabinet ministers, also soberly dressed.

Then the lights went out.

# CHAPTER 22

Pandemonium broke out. Candles were knocked to the floor. The odor of smoke and melting wax engulfed them. There was a real threat of clothing catching fire and people being trampled, as they stumbled and groped their way through the darkness. Fenimore hung on to Jennifer's hand with a fierce grip. The only things visible were the choir boys' white tunics, which glowed with a faint luminescence among the darker clothing.

As Fenimore and Jennifer emerged from the cathedral, a strong authoritative voice behind them shouted something in Czech. There were gasps and shocked expressions on all the faces around them.

"What's he saying?" Fenimore asked the people nearby. No one paid any attention to him. It was so frustrating not to be able to understand the language. It prevented him from pursuing his mission. He was stymied. A double wall of secrecy—the mystery itself and the language barrier were like a brick wall lined with a lead wall. He would penetrate the bricks, only to run up against the lead. He realized what it was like to be deaf: frustrated and isolated. He kept asking what had happened until someone who spoke English finally answered him: "The royal crown. It's been stolen!"

Fenimore stopped, causing Jennifer to stop, too. He still gripped her hand. He scanned the crowd. A few feet ahead, he had spied a large blonde woman, her hair pulled back with a comb. Her companion, a small, dark-haired man, turned at that moment and looked over his shoulder; he wore granny glasses and a trim goatee. The woman was lugging a bulging, blue tote bag that appeared to be heavy.

"See that couple?" Fenimore pointed them out to Jennifer.

She nodded, recognizing Ilsa at once.

"Don't let them out of your sight."

She nodded.

It was easy for Fenimore and Jennifer to stay out of sight in the crowd, but it was not easy to keep their quarry in view. They bobbed up and down, disappearing and reappearing. The strain of not losing them was intense. Fenimore kept his eyes on Ilsa's tote bag. As they approached the gates, the guards, who by now had been alerted to the theft, tried to prevent people from leaving. But there were not enough of them to hold the gates against the crowd. It overwhelmed them and reinforcements had not yet arrived. Ilsa and Redik made it through. Fenimore and Jennifer slipped out after them.

Once in the open plaza, there was more room and the crowd began to disperse. Redik paused to confer with Ilsa. They seemed to be having an argument over her tote bag. A mild tug-of-war ensued. They separated, heading in opposite directions. Ilsa turned back toward Golden Lane, and Redik continued straight ahead toward the steps that led down to Malá Strana. Redik had the tote bag.

"You follow Ilsa. I'll take Redik," Fenimore told Jennifer. "Don't let her see you. And *don't* confront her. Just find out where she goes. Then go back to the hotel. I'll meet you there." He hurried after Redik.

# CHAPTER 23

For once the weather report was accurate. It was a perfect day for the zoo. A few other people had thought so, too, Mrs. Doyle observed wryly, as she watched the steady stream of parents and children pouring through the wrought-iron gates.

Come on, kids. Let's pick up our tickets." She herded Marie and Horatio over to the ticket window. "Two tickets reserved for Dr. Fenimore?" she said politely.

The man smiled and after a brief search handed her a white envelope with the doctor's name on it.

"I'd like to buy one more," Mrs. Doyle said.

The man gave her another ticket. "That'll be twelve dollars."

Gracious, how prices had gone up! When she was a child, a trip to the zoo had cost one or two dollars at the most.

Once inside, Marie said, "Can we see the bears first?" She was clutching Jiri tightly.

Mrs. Doyle studied the zoo map that the cashier had given her with the tickets. The bears were located smack in the middle of the zoo grounds. "I think we'd better start at the beginning and visit the animals in order," she said. "Monkeys first, pachyderms next—"

"Huh?" Horatio looked up from his yo-yoing. Lately the toy seemed to be glued to his fingers.

"Elephants," Mrs. Doyle amended. "Then the lions, and tigers—and bears," she went on, unaware that she was quoting from *The Wizard of Oz*.

A brown arrow with MONKEYS printed on it in white letters pointed the way. Marie skipped ahead, while Horatio strolled behind. Mrs. Doyle followed more slowly, but was careful not to let them out of her sight. She couldn't rid herself of an uneasy feeling. That e-mail message from the doctor had been so strange.

After the elephants, Mrs. Doyle stopped at a vendor's stall and bought three boxes of Cracker Jack. No visit to the zoo would be complete without burrowing into the sticky, caramel-coated popcorn to find the prize at the bottom. Her father had always bought a box for each child. (Mrs. Doyle was one of a family of eight) and then they would all compare to see who had gotten the best prize. In retrospect she wondered why there hadn't been more fuss over the toys. She put it down to her father's personality. He had had that rare gift of maintaining discipline and good feeling at the same time.

For Marie, this was a new treat. She bored to the bottom of the box and came up with a tiny silver ring. As she slipped it on her pinky finger, she crowed with delight. It was a perfect fit.

Horatio pulled out a little silver frog with a slightly misshapen head. "Kid's stuff," he muttered, handing it to Marie.

Mrs. Doyle had to admit she was just a big kid. She was getting as much kick out of this as Marie was. Slowly, Mrs. Doyle reached in the box and drew out a miniature silver whistle. She pressed it to her lips and was thrilled when it produced a tiny *peep*. Marie clapped her hands. At a nearby drinking fountain, the nurse washed the whistle and gave it to the child.

As they moved on, Mrs. Doyle saw a scruffy-looking man staring at them. He was leaning against the railing that ringed the Otter Pond. When she caught his eye, he quickly looked away. Marie ran up to the rail and stared down at the otters. "Look," she cried, as one otter slid down the sliding-board and landed in the water with a splash. They watched the otters' antics for a while. When they moved on, the scruffy man had disappeared.

The next sign said BEARS, and Marie chatted with Jiri, in Czech, preparing him for the coming reunion with his relatives. Horatio resumed his yo-yoing. And Mrs. Doyle tried not to think about her feet.

# CHAPTER 24

Jennifer wove through the throng, stretching her neck from time to time to keep Ilsa's blonde head in sight. The other woman was moving rapidly down Golden Lane, as if on an urgent errand.

Golden Lane was a row of tiny stucco houses built during the reign of Rudolph II, when Bohemia still belonged to the Austrian-Hungarian Empire. According to legend, these houses were occupied by alchemists looking for a magic potion that would turn lead into gold. At one time, Franz Kafka had lived and written in one of these houses. Jennifer would have loved to linger there, but now was not the time to play tourist. She was on a mission.

At the bottom of the lane, Jennifer lost sight of Ilsa. She looked frantically to her right and her left, berating herself for even glancing at the quaint houses on Golden Lane. Finally she spied her quarry, slipping between the trees on the riverbank, heading toward a bridge. Not the Charles Bridge—another one, that was not as crowded.

Now Jennifer worried about her cover. There were only a few people crossing the bridge and if Ilsa turned, she would see her immediately. At the risk of losing her, Jennifer hung back. At one point Ilsa paused and glanced over her shoulder. Jennifer, who was about fifty feet behind her, leaned over the railing, pretending a deep fascination in a mallard duck. Ilsa had seen Jennifer once, and only for a minute, at a distance. They hadn't even been in the same room. But Jennifer had recognized Ilsa immediately. Why couldn't Ilsa do the same? Ilsa turned back and continued walking. Jennifer breathed easier. But she must be careful.

They continued their cat-and-mouse routine until Ilsa paused at a bus stop. This was not good. How could Jennifer get on the same bus with Ilsa without being seen? Answer: She couldn't. She would have to get a cab and follow the bus. But cabs were not plentiful in this neighborhood. In fact, Jennifer had not seen one since she had left the bridge. Impatient with the poor bus service, Ilsa moved on. Good. Jennifer prayed she would keep walking. The path they were following was lined with trees and thick shrubbery. If Ilsa decided to turn around, Jennifer could easily duck behind a tree or shrub. Ilsa didn't turn. She kept walking for three long blocks. The neighborhood began to change, from park-like to more urban. The trees grew sparser and some commercial buildings began to sprout up. A bank. A dress shop. On the next corner was a supermarket. Smaller than your average American market, but with a row of self-service carts lined up in front. To Jennifer's dismay, Ilsa went inside.

# CHAPTER 25

Redik moved fast. Fenimore had a hard time keeping up with him. His motion was like that of a dancer or acrobat—fluid and swift. Fenimore remembered that Redik had moved his marionettes with the same dexterity. The tote bag didn't hinder him.

The streets were full in Mala Strana. But the crowd had broken up into smaller clusters and people were talking excitedly about the theft. Fenimore understood a few exclamations. *"Zloděj!"* (*"Thief!"*) and *"Policie!"* (*"Police!"*), but most of it sounded like gibberish to him. Redik was heading for the Charles Bridge. Fenimore had no trouble keeping out of sight. Most of the people were heading in the same direction. He had trouble keeping Redik in sight, however. The man was wily, and disappeared easily. Midway across the bridge, Fenimore thought he had lost him. But he caught sight of him again near the Old Bridge Tower, the one he had climbed with Ilsa the day before. Keeping his eyes fixed on the back of Redik's head, he was startled to see him make a sharp turn into the tower. *Oh my god. How can I follow him now?* Fenimore hesitated, his hand on the door.

"You goin' up or what?" demanded an American tourist, draped in a backpack and multiple cameras.

"Uh. . . ."

"They tell me this is one of the best views of the city." The man pushed past him.

Fenimore followed cautiously.

# CHAPTER 26

The smaller brown bears were the ones that bore the closest resemblance to Jiri. Marie held the teddy bear over the rail and made him wave his paw vigorously. At one point the bear slipped and almost had a more intimate visit with his relatives. But Horatio reached out and grabbed him in the nick of time.

After watching the keeper feed the bears, Horatio announced, "I'm hungry."

"Me too," echoed Marie.

Mrs. Doyle escorted them to the picnic ground where they bought hot dogs, hamburgers, and sodas. When she saw the prices she fervently wished she had packed them a lunch. Too late now. They settled down on a bench at a long picnic table and removed the foil from their sandwiches. *At these prices, the foil should be sterling silver,* Mrs. Doyle thought, *and the sodas liquid gold.* As she took her first bite, she saw that man again. The one from the Otter Pond. He was eating at a table a few yards away. Well, that wasn't too unusual. People moved at a similar pace. It was the same in the supermarket; you kept running into the same shoppers over and over in the aisles. She relaxed and concentrated on her burger.

Horatio finished first and began playing with his yo-yo. He was so good at it, he attracted a little crowd of spectators. When he completed one especially elaborate trick, they even clapped. Mrs. Doyle was sorry he hadn't brought a hat. He could have set it out and collected enough to pay for their lunch.

After a while Horatio pocketed his toy and the crowd dispersed. Reluctant to get to her feet again, Mrs. Doyle prolonged her respite by eating slowly and sending the children off to buy ice cream. She was wrapping up their trash when she heard a commotion at the other end of the park. Quickly looking that way, she was horrified to see Horatio grappling with a man much bigger than himself. The man from the Otter Pond. To see Mrs. Doyle cover the ground between the table and Horatio, you would think she had the fittest feet in the universe. As she drew near, the man seemed to be getting the best of the boy. Marie cowered on a bench, eyes wide. Now and then she smacked her fist into her palm and cried, "Get him, Rat! Get him!"

Mrs. Doyle was about to enter the fray when Horatio freed himself and stepped back. There was a hiss, followed by a *thwack*, and the man fell to the ground.

Marie ran over to look at him.

"What's going on?" Mrs. Doyle grabbed each child by one arm.

"He tried to snatch Marie!" Horatio said, between pants. Sweat poured down his face, and, now that the danger was past, he looked scared.

"What in the world did you do to him?" Mrs. Doyle was relieved to see the man's foot move. For a minute she had been afraid—

"He hit him in the head with his yo-yo!" Marie stared at Horatio with awe.

"Good grief." Stirred by visions of David and Goliath, Mrs. Doyle patted the boy on the back. "Good for you, Rat!"

Turning, she saw a small crowd descending on them, a security guard leading the pack.

# CHAPTER 27

After Ilsa disappeared inside the market, Jennifer hesitated, hovering outside. If she went in, Ilsa might see her; but if she didn't, her quarry might leave by another exit. Curiosity won out over caution. Jennifer entered the store.

She spied Ilsa at the end of aisle 3. Cookies, crackers, pasta. Pretending to browse, Jennifer worked her way, crab-like, toward the opposite end of the aisle. Ilsa turned right. When Jennifer reached the end, she peered out in time to see Ilsa vanish through a swinging door. At first she thought it led outside. Then she saw the sign above it: ZÁCHOD The word meant nothing to Jennifer, but the silhouettes of a man and a woman below it were the universal sign for REST ROOMS.

Jennifer waited, her back to the sign, pretending to scrutinize the prices of beer and wine. Being able to buy alcohol in a supermarket was a novelty to Jennifer. In Philadelphia you had to go to a dreary state-owned liquor store that sold nothing but alcoholic beverages and related items. She kept her ears tuned for the sound of the swinging door opening behind her. A large family party, enjoying the adventure of shopping together, stopped directly behind her to discuss their purchases amid much hilarity.

When they finally moved on, Jennifer was afraid she had missed Ilsa. Had the woman come out while she was admiring the colorful wine labels? She looked swiftly around. No Ilsa. The next aisle was also empty. Her gaze was drawn to the front window, just as Ilsa appeared on the other side—striding away. She was empty-handed. Apparently she had not come to the store to buy anything, but merely to use the facilities. Jennifer would have liked to use them, too. But, like a good Hitchcockian heroine, she gritted her teeth and hurried after her prey.

# CHAPTER 28

Fenimore trudged up the tower steps behind the American tourist, pausing when he paused, climbing when he climbed. He hadn't the slightest idea what he would do when he reached the top. He would solve that problem when he got there.

The stairs were steep and seemed to go on forever. He hadn't remembered them being so steep or so numerous when he was with Ilsa. From time to time he glanced out the slit-like windows and glimpsed a slice of the city: red roofs, an emerald dome, or silver spires in the sun's ebbing rays. Now was not the time to admire the view. What *was* he going to do when he got to the top? Pretend to be touring, like that fellow ahead of him? *What a coincidence bumping into you, Redik,* he would say. *By the way, I just ran into Ilsa and she told me she'd like her tote bag back.*

Spying the statue of the tower guard, Fenimore paused. He was nearing the top. He heard the door to the roof open with a sound like a mewing cat. It fell shut with a thud. Redik and the tourist were up there together now. What were they doing—chatting about the view? Maybe the tourist was asking Redik to point out some of the outstanding buildings so he could photograph them. The tourist would then circle the roof, taking shots at odd and interesting angles, to impress the folks back home. This could go on for hours.

Fenimore examined the stone face of the tower guard more closely. There was nothing else to do. His face was pitted and worn from years of exposure to the weather. He must have been outside for many years. Fenimore wondered who had decided to bring him in. His thoughts turned inward. He began to fret about his friends. Would Jennifer listen to him and resist confronting Ilsa? His mind flew to Philadelphia. Were they getting along okay? Was Marie homesick?

*Creeeeak.* The roof door opened.

*Here he comes.* Fenimore's heart thumped loudly. *The tourist or Redik?*

"Nice," the tourist said. "I got some good shots." He patted one of his many cameras as he slipped past Fenimore.

Waiting until the man's footsteps faded away, Fenimore took a deep breath. Then he climbed the remaining stairs to the top of the tower.

# CHAPTER 29

As the security guard approached, Mrs. Doyle prepared what she was going to say. She still held Marie and Horatio, each by an arm. The man on the ground was beginning to stir.

"What's going on here?" The guard grabbed Horatio by the collar. The boy's dark skin, dark clothes, and youth automatically made him the most likely suspect.

"No, Officer. There's your villain!" Mrs. Doyle pointed at the man who was now trying to sit up.

"What. . . . What hit me?" The man succeeded in raising his torso and began rubbing his temple.

"He tried to snatch this little girl!" Mrs. Doyle cried.

While he sorted things out, the guard still held Horatio by the collar. A radio crackled on his belt. He spoke into it, asking for reinforcements. "What did you hit him with?" He gave Horatio a shake.

"My yo-yo."

"Give it here."

Reluctantly, the boy handed it over.

The guard examined it curiously.

The man was struggling to his feet.

"Don't let him get away!" Mrs. Doyle warned.

The guard pocketed the yo-yo and offered the struggling man his hand.

"That man tried to kidnap this child," Mrs. Doyle repeated in frustration.

The guard ignored her. "Are you all right?" he asked the man.

"A little dizzy." Now on his feet, the man continued to rub his temple.

Two other security guards joined them.

"This man needs medical attention. Take him to the first-aid station."

The newly arrived guard took the injured man's arm. The first guard started to march Horatio off.

"Wait—!" Mrs. Doyle cried.

Horatio sent a desperate look over his shoulder. The nurse was alarmed by his expression. She had never seen him look helpless and frightened.

"Where are you taking him?" Mrs. Doyle trotted behind, trying to keep up with them.

"The Main Office."

"I'm coming, too."

By way of an answer, the guard gave Horatio an unnecessary shove.

Holding on tightly to Marie's hand, Mrs. Doyle trailed after them. She racked her brain for some way to free the boy. If Dr. Fenimore were here, he would have thought of some—Wait a minute! Horatio would be allowed one phone call. An avid watcher of *Law & Order* Mrs. Doyle was sure of that. And she knew exactly who he should call.

# CHAPTER 30

Shadows were lengthening. Gaslights were flickering on. Jennifer was tired, hungry, and in desperate need of a bathroom. She trudged forward, keeping her eyes fixed on the large blonde woman in front of her who was plowing her way through the crowd—feeling like a tugboat in the wake of an ocean liner.

The wide boulevards had given way to a warren of narrow, twisted streets. This was an older part of the city. There were more people here. Young couples and tourists, mainly, out for a good time. Jennifer envied them. No worries—they could loiter, browse . . . and go to the bathroom whenever they felt like it!

She craned her neck, sighting the blonde head still bobbing above most of the others. Without warning, Ilsa turned into an alley and disappeared. *Now what?* Jennifer paused at the entrance and peered down the alley. Midway down, she saw Ilsa fitting a key into the lock of a wrought-iron gate. Stepping inside, Ilsa pulled it shut behind her with a clang.

Jennifer let a few minutes pass before she went up to the gate. Pretending to admire the delicate ironwork, she gave it a surreptitious tug. It was locked fast. Next to the gate, embedded in the plaster wall, was a yellow porcelain tile with the number 16 painted on it in black. As she left the alley, Jennifer carefully noted its name: LOUTKA ULIČKA. She had no idea what it meant. In the light of a street lamp, she flipped through her small Czech dictionary. *Loutka*: "doll, puppet." Then, *Ulička*: "alley." Doll Alley. Stowing the book, Jennifer dashed into the nearest café and accosted the first waitress she saw. *"Záchod!"* she said, making use of the word she had recently learned at the supermarket,

That emergency taken care of, she returned to Loutka Ulička. It was darker now but she could still make out the large, square house with plaster walls, tile roof, and twin brick chimneys—from the Renaissance period; a modern house by Prague standards. A strip of lawn bordered with flowerbeds lay between the gate and the house. In a few weeks those beds would burst into colorful bloom. Now they resembled newly prepared graves. Could this be where Fenimore's cousins were being held captive? Or was it simply Ilsa's home? Or a combination? It was too opulent to be the home of a professor, Jennifer decided. Was the locked gate the only entrance? She explored the adjacent alley to which the back of the house abutted. Nothing but a blank wall. No doors. Not even a window. Discouraged, she returned to the front gate. Topped with iron spikes, there was no chance of scaling it without risking serious injury. Desperately she scanned the alley, her gaze finally coming to rest at her feet. Beneath them lay an iron grate.

# CHAPTER 31

Fenimore slowly pulled open the door to the roof, trying by sheer willpower to prevent it from creaking. Carefully he drew the door closed behind him. Redik was nowhere in sight. He must be on the other side of the tower. Cautiously, Fenimore made his way along the narrow path between the tapering copper roof and the slim iron railing. Coming to the last bend in the path, Fenimore peered around the tower roof and saw him. His back to Fenimore, Redik was bending over the blue tote bag. As Fenimore watched, he reached inside and pulled something out. The royal crown. Its gems glowed red, yellow, blue, and green in the waning afternoon light. Redik gazed at it for a long moment, then placed it firmly on his head. Remembering the emperor's curse, Fenimore stifled a gasp.

With the crown perched at a rakish angle, Redik began to dance—a mincing two-step—not unlike one of his own puppets. His concentration was complete. Fenimore thought that even if he shouted, the man would not hear. Redik was in another world.

As he danced, he hummed. During one turn, his gaze was caught by the vista of Prague shimmering before him, silver and gold, like the crown. He paused, spreading his arms wide, as if trying to embrace the whole city. Wearing a voluptuous smirk—the expression of a greedy child who has just snatched a coveted toy from a play-mate—he slapped the crown on one side and cried, *"Můj!"* (*"Mine!"*) He removed the crown and cradled it against his chest. Gazing down at it, he murmured gently, "And this is only the beginning. . . ."

Fenimore had to strain to catch the words.

Redik raised his eyes once more to the view of the city and leaned over the rail. Gesturing with his free hand, he cried out, "Soon, you will be mine, too. All mine!"

Fenimore had no trouble translating the simple sentences. An unfamiliar sensation rose in his breast. A fierce, unreasoning rage. He rushed forward, reaching for the crown. Miscalculating, he fell against Redik, knocking the crown to the ground. They grappled for a moment. Redik lost his balance and began to topple. Fenimore clutched at the tail of his jacket, but it slipped from his grasp. The puppet master fell over the rail. His scream seared Fenimore like a flame. He hit the water with a dull smack that Fenimore barely heard.

But the people on the Charles Bridge heard it—young couples strolling, with eyes only for each other; older couples, arm in arm, musing on their past; artists absorbed in their sketches; and musicians engrossed in their notes. They all glanced up at the sound, just in time to see a man disappear beneath a jet of water.

Fenimore grabbed the crown, stuffed it in the tote bag, and ran down the stairs.

# CHAPTER 32

The Main Office of the zoo was dusty and overheated. Mrs. Doyle insisted on accompanying Horatio into the supervisor's office. She told Marie to sit in one of the metal chairs lining the wall. Marie obeyed, sitting quietly, eyes downcast, her small hands clasped in her lap. All the light and life had gone out of her face. Her features were waxen and still. Mrs. Doyle was reminded of a documentary film she had once seen of Jewish prisoners in Germany, awaiting their fate. *That's ridiculous. This is America!* "Marie!" she said.

The child looked up

"Everything's going to be all right." Mrs. Doyle made the AOK sign.

Marie looked away as if she didn't understand. She had been lied to by grown-ups before. Not her parents—others: teachers, her friends' parents . . . the super.

The supervisor asked the security guard to explain what happened. He did, eagerly laying all the blame on Horatio.

"That's not true!" Mrs. Doyle broke in.

"Quiet, please. You'll have your turn." The supervisor silenced her.

When Horatio was called on and asked for his side of the story, the boy spoke in a voice so low, Mrs. Doyle could barely hear him. The supervisor scribbled a few notes, then beckoned to Marie. She slid off her chair and came up to the desk.

"Can you tell me what happened just now at the picnic ground?" he asked

Marie spouted her story in rapid Czech. Under the stress of the moment, she had forgotten all her newly acquired English. The man frowned.

"Marie, sweetheart, speak English," Mrs. Doyle pleaded.

The child looked at her dumbly.

"You may sit down," the man said, not unkindly.

Uncomprehending, Marie remained standing until Mrs. Doyle gently led her back to her chair.

When it was Mrs. Doyle's turn to give her version, the supervisor dismissed it as hearsay evidence. She hadn't been there. She was merely repeating what the two children had told her. The supervisor then advised Horatio of his rights and told him he could make one phone call. The boy looked frantically around. Mrs. Doyle handed him a slip of paper on which she had written the number of the Police Administration Building, and Detective Rafferty's extension.

Rafferty was tidying up a routine assault-and-battery case when his phone rang. "Homicide. Rafferty speaking."

"It's Rat," a young male voice whispered.

"Rat? Speak up. Is this a crank call?"

Silence.

Rafferty was about to hang up when the voice of a woman, obviously at the end of her rope, replaced the boy's. "Detective Rafferty, this is Kathleen Doyle—"

"Oh, hi, Doyle. What's up?"

"Horatio is being held by a security guard here at the zoo, for assaulting a man with a yo-yo. . . ."

"Whoa. Start again."

"That's what happened. But the man he assaulted tried to kidnap Marie, Dr. Fenimore's little cousin, and—"

"Okay, okay." He stopped her in midsentence. "Put the security guard on."

There was a pause. Rafferty could hear raised voices in the background. Finally a sulky male voice came on the line. "Robinson here."

"Robinson. This is Detective Rafferty, Philadelphia Homicide. I want you to release Horatio Lopez, under my recognizance."

"But he—"

"Now!"

Silence.

"And, Robinson?"

"Yes sir?"

"Detain the injured party until I get there."

"On what grounds?"

"Attempted kidnapping."

"But . . ."

"I'll be right over." Rafferty slammed down the receiver, grabbed his jacket from the back of his chair, and headed for the elevator. He was thrilled to be doing some real police work for a change.

# CHAPTER 33

Jennifer stood looking down at the grate. It wasn't very big. About two feet by one and a half feet. Just big enough for a workman to slip through to repair a wire or fix a pipe.

*"Meow."*

The cat slid past Jennifer's ankle and sniffed at the grate. The bars were set too close together for even the smallest cat to squeeze through. Apparently that was the cat's intention. It rubbed its head against the grate and whined again.

*If only I had some tools,* thought Jennifer. *A crowbar and a sledge-hammer would be nice. A trifle noisy, but . . .* Bending down, she grabbed one of the bars and tentatively tugged on it. It shifted slightly. She set her purse on the ground and grabbed the bar with both hands. The grate rose an inch.

The cat, who had been watching her, turned its head toward the end of the alley. Its eyes shone bright amber. Jennifer turned to see the headlights of a car bearing down on them. She pressed herself flat against the fence. "Scat," she hissed, but might have saved her breath; the cat had already vanished. The car rolled past, missing Jennifer by inches. She waited until the taillights disappeared down the alley before tackling the grate again. This time, correctly gauging her strength against its weight, she shoved it to one side. Peering down into the dark cavity, she wished she had a flashlight. Wait. She did: the one attached to her key ring. While she rummaged in her purse, the cat reappeared. Without pause, it leapt into the open hole. Jennifer wished she could see how far the cat had gone, but her tiny flashlight beam was too weak to penetrate the darkness.

Two small marbles of light appeared. The cat was looking up to see if Jennifer would follow and its eyes were caught in her faint beam. Jennifer gauged the depth at about four feet. Without thinking, she jumped. The bottom was cement and stung her feet. Again the cat disappeared. But in which direction?

Jennifer reached out and touched a cool metal bar. Raising her hand, she touched another. A ladder was attached to the wall. How convenient. If necessary, she could make her escape. Uh-oh. What if another car came? Its wheel would get stuck in that hole. She had to replace the grate. She climbed the ladder and dragged the grate over the opening. And none too soon. A brilliant light illuminated the hole, as another car rolled over her. The light was accompanied by a loud thump. Jennifer had not replaced the grate carefully enough and the car had rocked it. But in that split second, while the hole had been lit up, she had glimpsed a passageway to her right. That must have been where the cat had gone. Yes, she heard it whining from that direction. She followed the sound. A slender bar of light gleamed at the end of the passage. The whining stopped.

*"Schlecte Katze!"* a female voice cried, and the light vanished.

*Bad cat!*—Jennifer had understood that. The words were not Czech, but German. And she had taken two years of German in college.

# CHAPTER 34

When Fenimore emerged from the tower a crowd was gathered at the end of the bridge—looking over the wall. He ran toward it.

"A man fell from the tower!" he cried in Czech, the language again coming easily to him in a crisis. He began to strip, preparing to jump in the water. Spotting a patrol boat nearby, Fenimore scrambled, in his underwear, onto the wall and began waving frantically. When the boat was near enough for the crew to hear, Fenimore called out, "Someone's drowning." As he spoke, Redik bobbed to the surface. Floating facedown, he lay still, making no effort to struggle or swim.

The captain of the patrol boat shouted an order and the boat drew neatly alongside Redik. It took three men to pull him aboard. Fenimore and the crowd watched in silence as the men took turns applying artificial respiration. Under the third man's ministrations, Redik stirred. A cheer went up from the crowd. Shivering in his undershorts, Fenimore watched them carry Redik into the cabin. Only then did he begin to put his clothes back on. He was reaching for the tote bag that contained the crown, when a voice behind him said, "You're under arrest."

•      •      •

Fenimore sat in the dank cell, watching a cockroach scuttle across the floor. He had not slept all night. His anxiety for his friends and for his cousins (not to mention the accommodations) had kept him awake. As the first gray light of dawn filtered through his cell window, it was hard not to feel depressed. His outlook was bleak. He was the only other person who had been in the tower when Redik fell. In a very real sense, he had caused the accident. And to top it off, he had been in possession of the stolen goods: the royal crown of Emperor Charles IV, no less. He shook his head.

Again he was reminded of Tomas Tuk, the towerkeeper. His accident had resembled Redik's—except Tuk was a much older man and had not survived the plunge. Fenimore shuddered. If Redik had been older and not as physically fit, Fenimore might be up for manslaughter—or even murder. When he got out of here, he resolved, he would look up Tuk's family and find out what had really happened to him.

A door clanged and he heard footsteps coming down the stone corridor. *This dungeon was probably built in the Middle Ages,* he thought morosely. All the Old World charms of ancient Prague had suddenly dimmed. He yearned to be in a spanking-new mall in the heart of Kansas.

The cockroach reappeared and, to Fenimore's eye, it had assumed the proportions of that insect in Kafka's famous story, *The Metamorphosis.*

# CHAPTER 35

When Rafferty entered the overheated office at the zoo, he was shocked by the appearance of his friends. Horatio, usually lounging casually with a lazy stare, sat rigidly upright, eyes wide, like an animal caught in the headlights' glare. Mrs. Doyle, always calm and tidy, was coming apart at the seams. Her neat bun had unraveled behind her ears, her coat was rumpled, and one shoelace was untied. The little girl sitting between them, pale and mute, reminded Rafferty of refugee children from Bosnia he had seen on the TV news.

As soon as they saw Rafferty, the boy and the nurse were transformed. Horatio's frozen look relaxed into his natural cool gaze. The worry lines around Mrs. Doyle's mouth melted into a broad smile. Marie was the only one who remained unchanged. She had never met Rafferty. To her, he was just another policeman, to be avoided and feared.

"What a happy party!" Rafferty clapped his hands. "All that's missing are the refreshments." He raised his already resonant voice. "Robinson?" The man he had spoken to on the phone poked his head out of his office. "How about bringing these fine people some coffee and Cokes, some pretzels and doughnuts? They're famished."

Robinson eyed him sullenly.

134

"I passed a couple of vending machines on my way in here. It won't take you a minute."

The supervisor called over his shoulder to his assistant, repeating Rafferty's request. A few minutes later his friends were sipping and munching contentedly, and looking very much revived. Little by little the story was retold.

The so-called victim was brought from the first-aid station, a piece of plaster decorating his scalp where Horatio's yo-yo had found its mark. He was uncommunicative, until Rafferty asked to see his immigration papers. Upon discovering that they had expired six months ago, the man became much more cooperative. He was suddenly eager to place the blame for his attempted kidnapping on foreign agents in the Czech Republic.

He admitted that he had been hired to snatch Marie and hold her until further notice. For this service, he was to receive $1,000. Unfortunately, he didn't know the names of his employers, only their e-mail addresses. And when Rafferty tried to contact them, his e-mail was returned with the cryptic message: DOMAIN UNKNOWN. He would get his more-accomplished FBI buddies to work on tracing them, but that would take time. There was no need to inconvenience his friends any longer, he decided. He extricated a release form from Robinson for Horatio, filled it out, and sent his friends home.

On his way out, Horatio remembered his yo-yo.

"Sorry, scout," Rafferty apologized, "you'll have to let that go. A small price to pay for your freedom, right?"

Horatio nodded, although he thought it was a high price.

Instead of returning home immediately, Mrs. Doyle decided to treat her two charges to dinner at the Silk City Diner. You would have thought she had suggested the Four Seasons. She didn't tell them she had chosen that diner because it was the only one in the city that she knew had a liquor license. After her experiences that day, she felt the least she deserved was a cold beer. After the waitress had recorded two Cokes for Horatio and Marie, Mrs. Doyle ordered a Budweiser.

Horatio looked up. "Make that two Buds."

Mrs. Doyle glared at him. "That'll be *one* Bud," she said firmly.

"Bud? What'sa Bud?" Marie looked up from placing a quarter in the jukebox, her mastery of English having magically returned.

The waitress left, looking flustered.

# CHAPTER 36

Ilsa was not stupid. After she let the cat in and fed him, she thought: *Why did he come to this door? How did he get here? There's no way he could get down here, unless . . . Had some careless worker forgotten to replace the grate?* She decided to investigate. She unlocked the door; thought better of it, and went to check something else first.

The cellar of the house was enormous, containing a network of vast rooms. In the old days of the Austro-Hungarian Empire, many of these rooms were used exclusively for storing wine. Later, during the Nazi occupation, one room was used by the gestapo for interrogating members of the Czech resistance. More recently, that same room had been used by the local police to question Communist backsliders.

Tonight this room served as a prison for two people—a man and a woman. They were both sedated. And the man was very ill. When Ilsa came in, the woman spoke to her. "My hush-band. . . . He needs . . . his medi-shin. *Bitte,*" she pleaded. She spoke German, because Ilsa preferred it. Her words came out haltingly and slurred because of the sedation.

"Not now. Later." Ilsa was impatient to examine the grate outside.

"The . . . presh-cription . . . ish . . . in . . . my . . . handbag," the woman persisted.

Ilsa shook her head. They had been through this before. "Not now." She reached for a glass on the table beside the cot. "Here, drink this."

"*Ne!*" The woman knocked the glass from her hand.

"Bitch." Ilsa slapped her.

The woman fell back with a groan.

Turning to leave, Ilsa ran into Jennifer.

A few minutes earlier, Jennifer had stood in the passageway outside the house, listening for sounds from within. After a while, when she heard nothing, she had tried the door. It opened easily into a dimly lit, low-ceilinged room with the rudiments of a kitchen—a small stove, a sink, a table, two chairs. No refrigerator. She decided to risk entering, hoping to eavesdrop on some useful conversation . . . or even, to find Fenimore's missing cousins. There was a dark, pantry-like recess near the door where she planned to retreat if she heard someone coming. She decided to investigate it now.

The recess led into another dark space that had another door. It opened to the reek of damp and mold. Inside, Jennifer's small flashlight could only pick out vague shapes. Zeroing in on one of these shapes, she found it was a sealed carton. She rummaged in her purse for something sharp with which to open it. Nail scissors. This would not be the first time *that* trusty tool had come to her aid. She went to work, digging and tearing. Inside were stacks of neatly bound folders. They looked like theater programs and, although they were in Czech, Jennifer could translate one word: *Loutka*. Doll.

What sort of program would have dolls in it? *Guys and Dolls?* Not likely in Prague. Ibsen's *A Doll's House?* Wait. Puppets *are* dolls. . . . A puppet show? Then she remembered: Andrew had told her that Redik was a puppeteer. Each pack of programs was for a different city in the Czech Republic; that much she could decipher.

Apparently Redik was planning a "Grand Tour." At the bottom of the box was a larger, single sheet, written in ink, by hand, and in German. As Jennifer began to translate, she grew puzzled. It seemed to be some kind of resolution or manifesto, regarding Prague. She tucked it in her purse, intending to study it later.

When she came to the end of the boxes, she turned her feeble beam on the room beyond. It appeared empty, but she decided to make sure. As she stepped around the boxes, she stumbled and almost fell into a hole. Playing her light over it, she judged it was about three feet wide, six feet long, and four feet deep. Casting the beam beyond the cavity, she picked out another hole, identical to the first. Deciding she had seen enough, she withdrew. When she reached the door, she directed her light on a paper sack in the corner. The large block letters spread across the bag were in Czech, but the illustration underneath conveyed the message aptly. It depicted a rodent, with crosses for eyes, its four feet sticking in the air.

Closing the door to the storage room, Jennifer moved along the wall and back into the kitchen. As she passed the sink, she grabbed a paring knife that was lying there. The quiet murmur of voices reached her. Slowly, she began to distinguish some words. To her relief they were not Czech, but German. The sound grew louder. Ilsa's angry cry, followed by a slap, propelled Jennifer through the doorway into the room. Ilsa turned and ran smack into her.

"You!" Ilsa fell back. "How did you get here?"

Jennifer only had time to see the cots bearing two prostrate forms, before Ilsa pushed her out of the room and shut the door behind her.

They faced each another.

*"Mew."* The cat came out of nowhere and curled around Ilsa's ankle. She shook it off, her gaze never leaving Jennifer.

"I followed you from the cathedral," Jennifer said simply. "I'm looking for Andrew's cousins." What was the point of lying? Ilsa wouldn't believe anything Jennifer told her, anyway.

"Andrew?" asked Ilsa.

Jennifer felt a small flush of triumph. The woman didn't know his first name. Their relationship couldn't have been *too* intimate. "Dr. Fenimore," she explained.

Ilsa's look of chagrin was brief. "You have made a mistake coming here," she said. "Now you must stay."

"Not necessarily." Jennifer chose this moment to brandish the paring knife.

Ilsa stepped back.

Silently, they eyed each other. Jennifer hadn't the slightest intention of using the knife unless Ilsa attacked first.

Sensing this, Ilsa relaxed a little. "Let's talk." She moved carefully across the room to the table and tentatively pulled out a chair.

"You first," Jennifer said.

Ilsa sat down.

Her eyes still on Ilsa, Jennifer took the chair opposite.

"Coffee?" Ilsa asked politely.

"No, thank you."

"Tea?"

Jennifer shook her head.

"Where is the doctor now?" Ilsa got down to business.

While thinking of her answer, Jennifer heard the muffled ring of a telephone. Ilsa opened a drawer in the table and took out a cell phone. "*Ja?*" Her gaze stayed on Jennifer. Except for a few grunts of surprise, Ilsa listened to her caller in silence. Finally, she said a few words in Czech, which Jennifer did not understand, and hung up. "So. Your *Andrew*"—she leaned on the name—"is in jail."

Jennifer felt cold.

"He tried to kill my friend." Ilsa glared at Jennifer. "He is being held for questioning." She smiled.

Jennifer remained silent, digesting her words.

"He pushed Jan off the bridge tower into the river. It's a miracle he survived." Becoming quite agitated, she stood up.

Jennifer rose, too, tightening her grip on the knife.

A sharp cry came from the next room. They both turned. The cry was repeated. Like two cats, they watched each other as together they moved toward the door.

When they entered the room, the man was bent over, holding his chest. The woman was leaning over the bed. She raised frightened eyes to them. "He is in great pain!"

Ilsa went to the cot. Jennifer followed close behind. Ilsa grabbed the man's hand and felt his wrist for his pulse. Jennifer and the other woman watched intently. Ilsa's anxious expression gradually disappeared. She dropped the man's hand. "He's all right."

*How do you know?* wondered Jennifer. At least Ilsa appeared relieved the man had a good pulse; that must mean she did not intend to kill him. At least—not yet. By this time Jennifer had guessed the identity of the man and woman: Fenimore's cousins. But this new knowledge was of no use to her. There was no way she could get the information to Fenimore. She was a prisoner.

This became clearer as the evening wore on. At some point Ilsa heated soup and produced a loaf of bread and cheese. She served small portions of these items to her guests. Vlasta did not eat. Anna and Jennifer did. Jennifer couldn't remember when she had last eaten. After this meager meal, she asked for a bathroom. Ilsa directed her to the pantry area. The little closet had no light, but Jennifer located the toilet easily by smell. There was a chain for flushing. About an hour later, tiring of her vigil, Ilsa rose and locked the back door; then the door to the cousins' room. Before ascending the back stairs (to the warm comforts of a feather bed, Jennifer thought ruefully), Ilsa paused and said sweetly, "Sleep well."

Jennifer heard the key turn in the door at the top of the stairs. She felt the paring knife in her jacket pocket. A lot of good *that* had done her! She kept her hand around it, however, as she settled down on a hard kitchen chair for the night.

# CHAPTER 37

Jennifer must have dozed off. She awoke with a start and realized a sound had awakened her—the sound of a voice . . . strident, but muffled by thick walls. The voice seemed to be giving a speech, but she couldn't make out the words. Remembering a trick she had used as a child to facilitate eavesdropping on the brawls of her neighbors in the adjoining apartment, she went to the cupboard and took out a drinking glass. She pressed the open mouth of the glass against the wall and her ear to the base. The sexless voice was ranting in German. It reminded her of Hitler's speeches in some movies that her teacher had shown to her German class in college. She pressed her ear against the base of the glass until it hurt. The voice grew louder, rising and repeating itself. She was able to translate two phrases that were repeated over and over:

*"Praha belongs to us!*
*We will rise again!"*

The last cry was followed by applause, punctuated by a few bravos. Then silence. A few minutes later Jennifer heard an outside door open, and footsteps. She turned out the little lamp on the kitchen table and went over to the barred window. It looked into the passageway through which she had come, but it was a tall window and if she scrunched down, she could see a bit of the lawn up above. She knelt in the dark kitchen, peering upward. The light of the single street lamp was enough to illuminate a series of feet filing out. One pair was a little ahead, leading the others. Jennifer heard the clang of the lock on the wrought-iron gate. She imagined the group disappearing down the alley. Soon, one pair of feet came back to the house. A woman's feet, wearing woman's shoes. Ilsa. Like many large women, Ilsa's feet were dainty and small. Jennifer let out the breath she had not realized she was holding.

What on earth? A rally of some sort? Of Redik's followers? Did he have a cult?

Jennifer tried to put the pieces together. There seemed to be more to this plan than a simple heist. The stacks of programs in the next room. *The room of the graves.* She shivered. The rally overhead. The two prisoners next door—probably Andrew's cousins. Could Redik and Ilsa be involved in a conspiracy of some kind? And were the puppets part of it? Andrew had told her how Czechs had used puppets in the past for subversive purposes. Could Redik and Ilsa have cell groups and be planning to overthrow the Czech government? *Good grief!* She had to warn someone. Andrew? Or President Hável? She looked wildly around the kitchen: at the single window with its iron bars, at the thick wooden door to the passageway with its secure lock, and at the other solid doors leading to various parts of the house—all securely locked. She was sweating and her breath came in short gasps.

Calm yourself. You're getting carried away. She forced herself to take deep breaths. It was probably a simple heist, after all. Those stacks of programs were just that—programs for Redik's traveling puppet shows. And that meeting upstairs—a town meeting to discuss some problem with the sewers or the transportation system. And those pits in the room next door? For trash disposal. Recycling.

*And I'm Marilyn Monroe!*

With a sigh, Jennifer slumped onto one of the kitchen chairs. But this time she didn't sleep.

# CHAPTER 38

The footsteps in the corridor came to a stop outside Fenimore's cell. A guard in a dark green uniform, a rifle slung over his shoulder, opened the lock.

"Come with me," he said.

Fenimore shuffled out and marched a few paces in front of the guard. In less than twelve hours, he had adopted the posture, gait, and resignation of a lifer. In a few more days he would also acquire the prison pallor.

They passed from the cellblock to an ordinary row of closed doors. The last door stood open. The guard ordered him to enter. Fenimore stood blinking under the bright overhead lights. An uniformed man with a carefully barbered moustache sat behind the desk. Another man, in street clothes, occupied a chair in front of the desk, his back to Fenimore. When the guard announced Fenimore, the latter man turned.

Redik.

The official with the moustache pointed Fenimore to an empty chair. "Sit," he said in Czech.

Fenimore sat. The guard remained by the door, at attention.

The official shuffled some papers on his desk. Took off his

glasses. Yawned. Stretched. Put his glasses back on. When he spoke, it was in a slow, measured drawl, reminding Fenimore of natives of the southern United States. "Mr. Redik . . . has decided . . . to drop all charges." He read from a paper on his desk.

Fenimore glanced at Redik. He was staring straight ahead, a faint smile playing about his lips. Could this passive, self-contained man be the maniac Fenimore had encountered on top of the tower a few hours ago?

"And," the official continued, "since you have returned the stolen goods"—the police had confiscated the crown when they arrested him—"the State, er, the Czech Republic will not press charges for the theft of the royal crown."

Fenimore blinked. Had he heard right? He could understand Redik's motive for dropping charges: Fenimore might bring kidnapping charges against him. But, "the State"?

"However . . ."

*Here it comes,* thought Fenimore.

The official removed his glasses and began polishing them with a dirty handkerchief. He put them on, and for the first time looked directly at Fenimore. "We still hold you responsible for the damage to the crown." Fenimore was fascinated by the way the light bounced off his lenses. "You will receive a bill for repair of the dent incurred when you dropped it—"

(When *who* dropped it?)

"And this bill must be paid immediately upon receipt." He shoved a form across the desk at Fenimore. "Please write your American street address, phone number, and e-mail address."

Fenimore carefully filled in the appropriate blanks, substituting Jennifer's e-mail address since he didn't have one (something he intended to remedy the minute he got home). He returned the form and waited for the axe to fall—his sentence of so many years at hard labor.

"You may go."

Bewildered, Fenimore looked at Redik—his face was impassive. Then at the guard; he was staring fixedly at the floor. Tentatively,

Fenimore pushed back his chair, with a scraping sound. Cautiously, he stood up. He knew all about the police getting your hopes up, only to squash them. It was a psychological technique. His mother had told him. . . .

Fenimore took a step toward the door. Another step. Another. The guard stood back to let him pass. He was in the corridor. He paused. Surely they would stop him now. It wasn't possible that he was free to go through that open doorway at the other end of the corridor. The one that was flooded with morning sunlight. He continued to put one foot in front of the other, all the time listening—for footsteps, shouts, gunshots—until he stepped outside. The sights and sounds of a busy commercial street on an ordinary workday rushed past him: the clanging trams, the chugging cars and trucks, the pedestrians striding by on their urgent errands. He stood on the steps, drinking it in—the sweet elixir of a free city, on a fresh morning, going about its business. Then he joined it, on an errand of his own.

He found a pay phone and, retrieving the scrap of paper on which he had scrawled Jennifer's hotel number, called her room. No answer. He tried the front desk. No messages. Now what? The last time he had seen her, she was following Ilsa. Where had Ilsa led her? To the University? Ilsa's home? Where was "home"? He consulted his pocket diary for the University number. He knew it was closed, but surely someone was on duty in the front office who could find Ilsa's home address for him. He dialed. A recording informed him that the University was closed for spring break from such-and-such a date to such-and-such a date. He hung up. Somewhere in that vast building there must be a human being, he told himself. Last time, he had found Redik! Fenimore would drop by. Taking out his guidebook, he consulted the map. The University was only a few blocks away.

The front door was open, but there was no one in sight. Not even the sweeper he had run into before. He was considering what to do next, when he heard the soft *tap, tap* of an old-fashioned typewriter.

The Czech Republic was not as high-tech as the United States; some of their typewriters still made noise. He followed the sound, which led him down a long hallway to an office door. There was no name on it, but it was ajar. He knocked.

"*Ano?*" A woman's voice.

He introduced himself and asked if she had a list of the professors' addresses and phone numbers. She asked him for some ID. The fact that he had a card stating that he was a cardiologist seemed to satisfy her. She produced a dog-eared booklet from a desk drawer. She watched him flip through it. Ilsa was listed at an apartment house on a street near the University. He jotted down the address. Then he looked for Redik's. To his disappointment, the only address listed for him was a box number. He returned the booklet. "*Děkuji.*"

The woman smiled and went back to her typing.

Ilsa's apartment house was shabby, badly in need of paint and repair. The upper half of the entrance door was glass but no one had been able to see through it for some time. The door was open. In the dusty, tiled vestibule, Fenimore scrutinized the battered mailboxes. Some were empty with no names attached. Locating I. TENÄCEK, he pressed the buzzer. He would wait three minutes, he told himself. While he waited, he thought about what to do next. He could wait here until another tenant came in or out, and try to slip past them. But it might be a long wait. And once he got inside he would probably be faced with another locked door: Ilsa's. For the first time he missed Horatio and his unique skills. He turned to go. But where?

Slow down, Fenimore. Think this through. He walked until he found a bench across from the Old Bridge Tower. There, he sat down and closed his eyes. The hum of traffic and the chatter of pedestrians coming to and from the Charles Bridge formed a soothing background for his turbulent thoughts. Methodically he went over the steps that had brought him to this point: why he had come to Prague, what had happened since he had arrived, and what he should do now.

1. He had come here to find out why his cousins didn't answer their telephone.
2. He had discovered Marie, his youngest cousin, in hiding, and learned from her that thugs had kidnapped his cousins.
3. In his search for his cousins he had met Redik, who had referred him to Ilsa . . .

Grimace.

4. . . . who had led him on a wild goose chase!
5. Which, in turn, had led him and Jennifer to St. Vitus Cathedral and one of the greatest heists of history.
6. Which had led to his pursuit of Redik, his near murder of same, and his ending up in prison . . .
7. and Jennifer chasing Ilsa, and ending up . . . where?

Dead end.

Goals: Find Jen. Find cousins. Find Redik and Ilsa—*and bring them to justice!*

Fenimore opened his eyes and stared at the blackened Bridge Tower. Wait a minute. You didn't go back far enough, Fenimore. What about Tuk? The tower guard who fell from that very roof to his death in the Vltava River. Maybe there was a connection. He looked up at the pinnacles behind which he had so recently stood. Tuk must have had a family. Maybe they could help. "Tuk" was an odd name. There couldn't be too many of them in Prague. Fenimore strode off, full of renewed purpose, to find a telephone book.

He found one at a pharmacy and riffled through the *T*'s. *Tuk, Tomas.* There it was. Reveling in his good luck, Fenimore hopped a tram to the man's district.

This apartment house was much grander than Ilsa's. From the Baroque period, its stone facade was enlivened by a variety of winged creatures—doves, swans, cupids, angels. He had to hunt for the mailboxes. Of polished brass, they gleamed discreetly in a corner of the spacious lobby. Spying the name A. TUK, he turned to the desk, where a stern concierge eyed him coldly. Fenimore gave the name and cursed himself for not calling the Tuks from a pay phone first.

"Ms. Tuk will speak with you." The concierge handed him the house phone receiver.

"*Ano?*" A metallic female voice.

He explained who he was and why he had come, as well as he could in Czech. Switching easily to English, the woman asked him to wait a minute. She was gone so long Fenimore thought she had forgotten him. Finally her voice spoke: "My mother will see you. We are on the fifth floor, apartment five-oh-three."

The fragrance of Czech cooking leaked from under the apartment door. A smartly dressed woman let him in. Surveying him briefly, she said, "My name is Alicia. My mother speaks no English, but I will be glad to interpret for you."

Fenimore thanked her.

She led him through a large living room, expensively furnished in a modern decor—all mirrors, glass, and chrome. She stopped in front of a soft dumpling of a woman who looked up at him quiz-zically from an uncomfortable, angular chair. "My mother, Mrs. Tuk." Alicia introduced her. On closer inspection, Fenimore saw that Mrs. Tuk was a sad and wizened dumpling.

They drew up chairs and Fenimore began his interrogation. Mrs. Tuk was a willing subject. It was as if all her thoughts and feelings about her husband's death had been bottled up and Fenimore had pulled the cork. She told him about the man who had come to the tower every evening, just before closing. How he had stared out at the city of Prague, ranting and raving—sometimes even dancing! Her husband had to ask him to leave several times. And once the man had become violent, shoving her husband against the rail and swearing at him. That night he had arrived home shaken, she re-membered.

"Did your husband ever describe this man?" asked Fenimore.

She was thoughtful. "Small and dark," she finally said.

"You never told me all this," Alicia said peevishly.

Her mother muttered something that Alicia did not translate. Fenimore thought it sounded like, "You were too busy."

Deciding he had learned all he could, Fenimore rose and thanked the two women.

Mrs. Tuk sent her daughter a glance.

Alicia asked, "Won't you stay for lunch?"

Inhaling the divine odors wafting from the kitchen, Fenimore was sorely tempted, but he graciously declined.

Once back on the street, he thought, *That was all very interesting, but it doesn't bring me any closer to finding Jen.* A poster on a nearby kiosk advertising Redik's puppet show gave him an idea.

# CHAPTER 39

FBI geeks are good at tracking down felons via the Internet. Within twenty-four hours Rafferty had Redik's e-mail address on his desk, and from that he was able to locate his street address: 16 Loutka Ulička, Prague, Czech Republic. He called Mrs. Doyle to find out where Fenimore was staying so he could relay the message to him by phone or e-mail. The nurse provided the information. But there was no answer to Rafferty's repeated phone calls. And Redik's address lay unknown in his cousins' computer inbox. The detective began to grow concerned.

So did Mrs. Doyle. She had sent a number of messages to the doctor, telling him about their exploits at the zoo, and received no answer. And now Rafferty was having the same experience. Perhaps the Borovys' computer had crashed. Being a novice, maybe the doctor had busted it. But why didn't he answer the phone? Was he afraid it was being tapped?

Horatio, a sensitive youth under his seemingly tough exterior, sensed something was wrong. When he came in at the usual time, he took one look at Mrs. Doyle and said, "Heard from the doc?"

She shook her head.

Marie, hearing Horatio's voice, ran out from the kitchen. "Look,

Rat! We made cookies." She handed him a sugar cookie that bore a vague resemblance to a rabbit. Horatio bit off one ear. Although it tasted like cardboard, he grinned and licked his lips. "Yum," he said.

Marie glowed.

Mrs. Doyle remained preoccupied.

"How 'bout gettin' me another?" The boy nudged Marie. She ran back to the kitchen.

"He doesn't answer the phone or his e-mail," she confided to Horatio in a low voice.

"He's probably having a good time—seeing the sights. And now that his girlfriend's over there—maybe he's staying at her place." He winked.

Doyle, her romantic instincts stimulated, smiled. That was possible. But, no—he was on a mission. The doctor would never abandon his cousins in pursuit of pleasure. She frowned. "I don't think so."

Marie came running back.

*Doesn't that child ever walk?* Mrs. Doyle thought irritably.

Marie handed Horatio an elephant, complete with trunk and tail. "Pat-a-drum," she said confidently.

"Pachyderm," the boy corrected her.

*You tell that boy something once, and he never forgets it,* Mrs. Doyle noted with envy. Her own memory wasn't as good as it used to be.

Horatio bit off the tail of his cookie, munched, and raised his eyebrows.

Marie giggled.

Before he began on the trunk, Mrs. Doyle went in search of an aspirin.

# CHAPTER 40

Jennifer dozed fitfully on her kitchen chair, awakened sporadically by the muffled groans of Vlasta, reminding her of his suffering. As soon as Ilsa appeared the next morning, Jennifer faced her. "That man belongs in a hospital!"

Ilsa frowned. But she did not deny it. When they went in, Anna was sitting on the edge of her cot, looking pale and drained. Her eyes were fixed on Jennifer—obviously wary: Who was she? Where did she come from? And most important, whose side was she on?

Jennifer attempted to reassure her with a tentative smile.

Encouraged, Anna spoke up, looking directly at Jennifer. "My husband needs his medicine. The prescrip-sh—"

*"Ja, ja,"* Ilsa cut in impatiently. But she picked up a handbag from the floor and brought it to Anna. Anna rummaged through it and pulled out a piece of paper. Ilsa snatched it from her and went into the kitchen. Jennifer and Anna listened silently to Ilsa's side of the phone conversation. Anna recognized the word *"lékárna,"* and her face brightened. "Pharmacy," she translated for Jennifer.

*But do they deliver?* Jennifer wondered. *"Ich bin freund von Dr. Fenimore,"* she whispered to Anna.

Her eyes widened. But Anna was inclined to believe her, because

Jennifer's German was tinged with an American accent.

Ilsa came back. She glanced nervously at the man lying on the cot. He had not stirred since she left. Her gaze passed to Jennifer and Anna. "What have you two been plotting?" She glanced at the knife still in Jennifer's hand.

The women didn't answer.

"Well, I've ordered the medicine. It will be here soon."

There was the faint sound of a bell in a distant part of the house. Ilsa looked startled. Too soon for the medicine. She was obviously uncertain what to do next and didn't want to leave Jennifer alone with Anna. But she had to answer the door. "Come with me," she ordered Jennifer.

Jennifer looked at Anna. The woman nodded. She followed Ilsa to the door that opened to the back stairs. They both went up. Ilsa glanced back to make sure Jennifer was there, before opening the door at the top. They stepped into a dim, lofty room smelling of must and camphor. Bulky, shrouded furniture rested on an Oriental rug. In one corner stood a grand piano. From the ceiling hung a crystal chandelier, badly in need of a wash. Blinds covered the tall windows. The heavy front door—of oak, probably—bore an ornate wrought-iron lock.

"Stay here." Ilsa stopped Jennifer at the head of the stairs and moved silently toward the window. Pulling the blind-cord, she opened the slats a sliver and peered out. The bell rang again— sounding much louder this time.

"Open up! It's me."

Ilsa rushed to undo the lock. Redik darted in. "What took you so long?" he asked.

"Hush." She directed his gaze at Jennifer.

"*Kdo?*" ("*Who?*")

"Dr. Fenimore's *Mädchen*," Ilsa said.

"Oh, *Mûj Boże!*" ("*Oh, My God!*")

Jennifer almost smiled at his obvious consternation. But it was not a situation for smiling. She fingered the knife. Would she be able to hold off the two of them with such a small weapon? The odds were against it. They had moved away from the door, over to the piano, and were conferring in low tones.

"There's a sick man downstairs," Jennifer said impatiently. "He needs medical attention."

Ignoring her, they continued their conference.

"Where is Dr. Fenimore?" she asked loudly.

Redik glanced up, annoyed by the interruption. Ilsa came toward her. Redik followed. And Jennifer knew they were going to try to take the knife.

# CHAPTER 41

The he theater was closed, of course. The sign in the ticket window read: OTEVŘENO—3:00 P.M. It was only one-thirty. But there must be a watchman. Fenimore looked for a buzzer or bell. He found one beside the ticket office door. After a long wait, he heard footsteps and an elderly man appeared. *Zavřeno*, he mouthed through the glass: *Closed*.

*Pohotovost*, Fenimore mouthed back: *Emergency*. "I left an important notebook in Redik's dressing room," he said in English.

The man shook his head, indicating he didn't understand English.

Fenimore took out his wallet. The man's eyes brightened. But to Fenimore's dismay, his wallet was empty. The super had cleaned him out. And he had never made it to the American Express office to cash more traveler's checks. "I'll be right back," he shouted through the glass.

The man turned away.

Fenimore returned with the cash in less than fifteen minutes. He had run all the way. He hit the buzzer again. This time the wait was much shorter. The man let him in. Fenimore gave him three hundred korunas, the equivalent of ten American dollars. The man actually smiled, revealing three teeth. Dental care in the Czech Republic still left much to be desired.

Fenimore passed through the dim lobby into the darker theater. The door, through which Ilsa had led him the night before, was not locked, and he easily found Redik's dressing room. Now, if it would only be open. He tried the knob. It wouldn't turn. Damn. More money. More time lost. He hurried back to the lobby. It was empty. The smell of cigar smoke drew him behind the cloakroom to the watchman's lair. Slouched in a battered armchair, he was reading a newspaper and puffing on a cigar.

Fenimore explained about the dressing room door in pantomime—as if acting out a charade.

The man showed no interest, engrossed in his newspaper.

Sighing, Fenimore again reached for his wallet.

Once inside the dressing room, Fenimore waited until the watchman's footsteps faded away before he began his search.

He yanked the pillows off the couch and felt in the cracks. All he came up with were a piece of hard candy, some coins, and a bit of purple ribbon. The drawer in the table contained a pack of stale cigarettes and three matchbooks. He studied the matchbooks. All from the same place—Café Slavia. Redik must be a regular customer. If all else failed, Fenimore could hang out at the café every evening until Redik came in. He moved on to the closet. This looked more promising. It was crammed with wooden cases and boxes. But, after carefully examining each of them, the only address he found was that damned box number. He returned everything to its place and scanned the room one last time. Nothing. Discouraged, he closed the door behind him.

He was starting up the dark aisle, past the rows of empty seats, when he remembered something. *The puppets are kept in a cupboard behind the stage,* Redik had said. *They are so fragile, we don't like to move them any more than necessary.*

Fenimore bounded onto the stage and slipped through the heavy velvet curtain. At the back of the stage hung another, lighter curtain. He pulled it aside. There was the cupboard. Was it locked, too?

Yes, but the key was in the lock. Fenimore turned it. There they were. Hanging side by side from pegs, staring blankly at him with their gargantuan eyes.

There is something eerie about a puppet hanging limp and lifeless after a performance. Once the animation and the animator are gone, it is like a little death. Unlike a live actor who merely leaves his costume and makeup behind, the puppet leaves his heart—and soul. In turn, the puppeteer gets a false sense of power. Not only does he make his puppets perform, he infuses them with life—like God.

No help there, Fenimore decided. Abruptly, he changed his mind. Taking out a miniature flashlight attached to his key ring, which Jen had given him, he began to examine each marionette minutely—one by one. He stared intently at their finely carved faces, their miniature hands and feet. He felt their silk dresses, velvet cloaks, and suits. Of course, the most exquisite puppet was the emperor Charles IV. He wasn't wearing his crown. That was too delicate; it had to be carefully packed away after every performance. But he was wearing his beautifully crafted leather boots and his velvet robe of midnight blue trimmed with ermine. Fenimore admired the fur collar and cuffs. Then, like a voyeur, he peered under the cloak. Something white caught his eye. Sewed to the center seam at the back was a tiny label. He shined the flashlight beam on it, and read:

16 Loutka Ulička
PRAHA

Elated, he jotted the address down in his notebook. Then he had doubts. Was this the address of Redik's home—or just some puppet shop?

*"What are you doing?"* The shrill treble voice sliced through the theater.

Fenimore turned. Ema, Redik's intern—face flushed, lips trembling—was bearing down on him.

"I'm sorry. I'm afraid my curiosity got the better of me. I had to see these magnificent—"

"How did you get in here?" Her voice pierced the air like a stiletto.

"How did *you* get in?" Fenimore stalled her, trying to come up with a plausible excuse.

"The stage door. I have a key." Her voice dropped a notch—from stiletto to dagger.

"I was passing by and I had to see these beautiful objects up close. I knew I wouldn't have another chance. I leave for America soon."

Squinting at him in the poor light, she said, "You're the man who was in the dressing room." Her expression softened and her gaze shifted to the puppets. "Yes, they are beautiful." She lifted Kasparek from his peg. "He is my favorite. Always into mischief, aren't you, my pet?" She patted his rump. Her voice, when speaking to the puppet, was quite different, Fenimore noted. Like a moth brushing the ear.

"Well, I must be going. I'm sorry I upset you."

She smiled. "I'm sorry I lashed out at you. They are very delicate, you know."

"By the way," he turned back, "could you give me Mr. Redik's address? I'd like to write and tell him how much I enjoyed his performance."

"You can send it to the University. That's the only address I know."

He left her conversing with the puppets—as if with her friends.

# CHAPTER 42

Still no mail?" asked Mr. Nicholson, observing Mrs. Doyle's dejected expression.

"Not a thing. I can't understand it. I'm really worried." she said, then wished she could bite off her tongue. She knew he hadn't heard from Jennifer either.

Mrs. Doyle had come over to the bookstore early to use the computer, bringing Marie with her. Full of hope and expectation, the nurse had been confronted by an empty screen.

"Have you tried telephoning?"

For the moment, Marie was occupied with picture books in a far corner of the store. "Yes. They don't answer," she said.

The bookseller was at a loss for further suggestions.

"If it weren't for Marie, I'd have half a mind to go over there myself and see what's going on," Mrs. Doyle said.

Mr. Nicholson cast a quick glance at the little girl—her head bent over a book. She looked much like Jennifer had looked at that age. "I could keep her," he said impulsively.

"Oh, no. That's very kind but . . ."

"Seriously. I raised a daughter single-handedly, you know."

"Oh, I don't doubt your competence, Mr. Nicholson—but I wouldn't want to impose."

"Horatio's still on vacation, isn't he? He could give me a hand while I'm minding the store."

"Well, I. . . ."

"Besides, I have an ulterior motive." He fixed her with a serious gaze. "I'm worried about Jennifer."

"Well, if you put it that way . . ." Mrs. Doyle said.

Once again Detective Rafferty's services were required. It was he who arranged her plane ticket, and her transportation to the airport. (Fortunately she had a passport from past vacation travels.) As evidence of his efficiency, the nurse found herself staring down at the vanishing lights of Philadelphia's skyline just four hours after she made her decision to leave.

# CHAPTER 43

As Ilsa and Redik advanced on Jennifer, she tightened her grip on the knife. Would she have the nerve to use it? She had never deliberately harmed anyone. She steeled herself.

The doorbell rang.

Saved by the bell. Jennifer repressed a hysterical giggle.

Ilsa opened the door and took in the small white envelope. Without a word, she went down the stone steps to the basement. Jennifer waited, watching Redik. He indicated she should go down after Ilsa. He followed her.

When they came into the room, Vlasta was sitting up, clutching his chest, his face strained and white. Anna stood by helplessly.

Redik, unconcerned, disappeared into the kitchen. They heard the water running in the kettle. Was he actually making himself tea, Jennifer wondered? Ilsa took a pill from the envelope and reached for the glass by the cot. Anna shook her head. "No water. These go under the tongue." She gave the pill to her husband. He placed it under his tongue and fell back.

"We have to get him to a hospital," Jennifer repeated.

For the first time, Ilsa looked disconcerted. She went into the kitchen and Jennifer could hear her speaking urgently to Redik. Staring at Vlasta's waxen features, Jennifer thought, *They'd better not waste any time.*

As if echoing her thoughts, Anna began to cry softly.

# CHAPTER 44

Fenimore had no trouble locating 16 Loutka Ulička. He stood in front of the wrought-iron gate as Jennifer had before him. He stared at the desolate flowerbeds and tugged on the gate to see if it was locked. But, unlike Jennifer, he did not look down at the grate under his feet. Instead, he ran his hands over every inch of the gate searching for a buzzer or bell. He found one—a button—cunningly concealed behind an iron floret. The bell would have been of no use to Jennifer, however, because she had wanted to keep her presence concealed—like the button. Fenimore didn't care.

In the basement of the house, once again they heard the bell ringing faintly overhead. Ilsa cast a frightened look at Redik. "Police?"

Redik paused, his teacup halfway to his mouth.

They remained immobile.

"I'll go," Jennifer said, brightly.

Her words galvanized them. Ilsa started for the stairs. Carefully setting down his cup, Redik went after her.

Feeling like the perennial sheep, Jennifer followed them.

Upstairs, the previous ritual was repeated. Only, this time, it was Redik who opened the blinds a sliver and peered out. "It's him."

Although he spoke in Czech, the meaning of his words was clear to Jennifer. The gloom was too thick for her to see if he turned pale. Who was the "him"? Did she dare hope . . . ?

Ilsa came over and looked out. Turning quickly from the window, she said, "What now?"

"Don't answer," said Redik.

"What about him?" She nodded at the floor, referring to the other "him"—the one in the basement. "What if he dies?" She was becoming agitated. "We are responsible." Her voice rose. "I never agreed to this!" she cried.

"Quiet," he snapped, glancing at Jennifer.

"Don't worry about her. She doesn't understand anything. Americans are dunces. They speak only one language—English."

Redik was thinking hard. Finally he said, "Maybe we can work something out. I have something on him; he has something on me. Tit for tat."

Ilsa looked skeptical.

The bell rang again.

"Let him in."

"Are you sure?"

"Ano," he spoke sharply.

In the end, Redik ran the show, Jennifer noted.

Ilsa opened the door and went out to the gate.

# CHAPTER 45

Mrs. Doyle disembarked from the plane, stood passively by while her belongings were ransacked, and presented her passport to the Czech official. (She looked a fright in that picture. She had hardly had time to comb her hair!) Clutching the address of the doctor's cousins tightly in one gloved hand, she went to hunt up a cab.

She realized that she was probably on a fool's errand. If no one was at the apartment, how would she get in? She should have brought Horatio, she thought wryly. That unsuspecting youth had no idea how often his services were desired, and by how many.

Mrs. Doyle was so preoccupied, she hardly noticed the scenery as she passed. She would look at it later, she told herself, when she didn't have so much on her mind.

The cab pulled up in front of a nice apartment building—all gray stone and green awnings. She carefully counted out the correct number of korunas. (Rafferty had exchanged enough cash into korunas to carry her for a few days.) "Wait for me, please," she told the cab driver, never doubting that he understood English—which he did. He nodded and stayed put.

Mrs. Doyle went into the foyer, found the apartment number,

and pressed the buzzer. No answer. She pressed again. While she waited, the inner door opened and a man stepped out.

"Oh, thank you." Mrs. Doyle smiled pleasantly and stepped inside. The man looked surprised but let the door fall shut behind him. The hall was empty and silent. She sniffed, inhaling a mixture of scents; the residue of thousands of meals cooked by past and present residents. She padded down the hall until she came to number 1E. She tapped on the door. Nothing. She knocked louder. Still nothing. Although she hadn't expected anyone to be there, she was deeply disappointed. She retraced her steps and got into the cab. She asked the driver to take her to a moderately priced hotel. The source of her daily travel funds was the office cashbox, and she had to be careful. She sat back, closed her eyes, and tried to think what to do next.

# CHAPTER 46

Fenimore watched the front door of the Renaissance house intently. When it opened and Ilsa stepped out, he closed his eyes briefly. Why did it still surprise him when evil came in nice packages? Would he never learn? Remembering Pinocchio, he was amazed that her nose was still the same size.

She came briskly up the path, but had the decency to avoid his eyes as she unlocked the gate. Neither spoke. What was there to say? He followed her back to the house.

By the time they entered, Redik had relieved Jennifer of her paring knife. She had underestimated him. Because he was small, she had assumed he was also weak. He had taken the knife from her as if it were greased with butter. Now it was in his pocket and he held her arms behind her back in a strong grip.

Taking in the situation, Fenimore grinned. "Hi, Jen."

"Hi!" She grinned back. Despite her awkward position she felt a warm flow of relief.

Rattled by this nonchalant exchange, Ilsa's eyes narrowed, her gaze sliding from one to the other.

Redik, retaining his grasp on Jennifer, said to Fenimore, "As you Americans say, 'Let's make a deal.'"

Fenimore stared, expressionless.

"I will let your cousin go to the hospital, if . . ."

Fenimore glanced at Jennifer.

"He's very ill," she said.

". . . *if* you promise to leave us alone. No police. No investigation. No retribution," he finished.

"Let her go," Fenimore demanded.

"Not until you agree to my proposition." He gave her arms an extra twist.

Jennifer winced.

"So help me—" Fenimore started toward him.

"Stop." Ilsa stepped between them. "Let's sit down and talk this over like civilized human beings. Come. . . ." As she turned, she tossed Fenimore a coquettish glance.

Fenimore felt a surge of nausea.

Redik shoved Jennifer toward the stairs, then nodded at Fenimore. "You two go first," he said. Ilsa followed. And Redik brought up the rear. In the kitchen, there were only two chairs. Redik pushed Jennifer into one and stood behind her. He told Ilsa, "Take him to see his cousins."

She looked alarmed.

"Do it."

She gestured for Fenimore to follow her.

They weren't gone long. When Fenimore came back, his face had lost its natural color and his expression was grim. "Where is the telephone?"

"Have you decided?" Redik asked.

Fenimore gave a curt nod.

Jennifer looked away.

Ilsa drew the cell phone from the drawer in the table and handed it to Fenimore. They all watched him dial the Czech equivalent of 911.

While they waited for the ambulance to come, everyone was silent except Redik. He hummed an aria from *The Magic Flute* and stroked his cat. Everything was going his way.

"Tomas Tuk," Fenimore said, abruptly.

Redik glanced up.

Fenimore met his stare.

Redik dropped the cat and gave it a mean shove with his foot.

Fenimore relaxed. He had tipped the scale.

While they waited in the kitchen for the ambulance, Fenimore decided it was time to get a few things straight. "Why did you kidnap my cousins?"

Redik and Ilsa remained mute.

"Was it for their knowledge of the cathedral and the secret passage to the crown jewels?"

The pair appeared startled.

"Speaking of that—where is the manuscript you stole?" For the first time, Fenimore looked directly at Ilsa. "You can have no use for it now."

With a jerk of his head, Redik indicated that Ilsa should bring the manuscript.

She disappeared. Returning shortly, she handed it to Fenimore. A cursory look reassured him that it was unharmed. He tucked it under one arm.

"Now *I* have a question," Redik said.

Fenimore waited.

"Where was the child hiding?"

Fenimore suppressed a smile. Remembering the Czech word for porcelain stove, he spoke it softly, *"Kamna."*

Their looks of dismay were worth all the hours he had spent with the Richard Scarry picture book.

"We almost had her at the zoo!" Ilsa blurted.

Fenimore peered at her.

"Hush!" Redik hissed.

Earlier, when Ilsa had ushered Fenimore into the room where his cousins were confined, the first thing Anna had said to him was not "Thank God!" or "Help us!" but "Is Marie all right?" And he had been able to reassure her. Now he began to have doubts.

The sound of an ambulance siren filled the kitchen.

# CHAPTER 47

The house seemed strangely quiet after they had gone. Ilsa moved restlessly around the big living room. Finally settling at the piano, she picked out the same tune over and over with two fingers. She was still smarting from Fenimore's look of disgust when she had smiled at him.

Redik went to the closet and took out his favorite marionette—Charles IV—a shabbier version than the one he used at the theater. Also, an older version. It had been his puppet as a child, and his father's and grandfather's before him. In fact, it had been created by his great-grandfather, who had been a stonemason.

He manipulated the strings deftly, making the emperor perform a little two-step on top of the piano.

Without looking up, Ilsa said quietly, "Who is Tomas Tuk?"

As if deaf, Redik continued to play with his puppet.

Ilsa pressed her palm down sharply on the lower keys. The heavy, discordant notes vibrated through the house.

When the sound petered out, Redik laid the puppet gently on the piano and took a seat beside Ilsa. He began to play a Mozart concerto. He played very well. When he finished, Ilsa laid a hand over his.

He turned toward her. "Tomas Tuk is nothing to you." He reached up and twisted a strand of her hair around his finger. "And Fenimore and his *Mädchen* will never leave Prague."

Ilsa's eyebrows rose.

"You need not be involved." He let her hair uncurl and drew his finger down her cheek. "I know your sensibilities are too delicate. . . ."

She pushed his hand away, and looked at him—as if for the first time.

"Just leave it to me," he said. "Prague *will* be ours!" He turned back to the keyboard. This time he played a vigorous German march.

# CHAPTER 48

Horatio, Marie, and Mr. Nicholson were watching cartoons on the bookseller's television set in his apartment over the store. Such colorful images had never graced his screen before. Black-and-white Hitchcock films and the lovely faces of Grace Kelly and Ingrid Bergman were what usually flickered there.

As he watched, Mr. Nicholson couldn't prevent an occasional ejaculation, such as, "Goodness!" "Mercy" or "My word!" But his companions seemed unmoved—or mesmerized.

During a commercial break, Horatio said, "I wonder what they're up to now." He didn't have to explain to whom he was referring. The Doctor, Jennifer, and Mrs. Doyle were foremost in all their minds.

Mr. Nicholson glanced at his watch and did a swift calculation. "It's seven P.M. here, so it must be one A.M. there. I imagine they're sleeping peacefully."

"Mama and Papa, too?" asked Marie, out of the blue. She hadn't mentioned her parents since she had arrived.

Mr. Nicholson nodded gravely. "Mama and Papa, too."

Horatio cast him a quick glance. But the commercial break was over and the bookseller's gaze was back on the screen.

In a few hours they, too, would be sleeping peacefully. Mr. Nicholson in his own bed; Marie in Jennifer's bed; and Horatio on the couch. His mother had given the boy permission to stay over, so he could baby-sit with Marie the next day while Mr. Nicholson ran the store. Mrs. Lopez knew her son would never get up early enough to be at the store when it opened.

# CHAPTER 49

The hotel that the cab driver had picked out for Mrs. Doyle was modest, but neat and clean. The building had once been a convent, the brochure claimed. Here and there, reminders of its past peeked through the modern veneer. A marble statue, a wrought-iron railing, a Gothic window.

After she had settled in—washed up, and put her few things away—she decided to call some of the other hotels and see if Jennifer was registered. Not for the first time, she wished Jennifer had left her address with someone at home. If not with Mrs. Doyle, at least with her father. Then again, she was probably in such a hurry, she forgot. But when Mrs. Doyle opened the phone book to "Hotels" she was daunted. There were so many, it would take her days to cover them all. And it would be just her luck to have Jennifer staying in one that began with $Y$ or $Z$. She decided to start with the hospitals. There were only three of them. Maybe the doctor or Jennifer had met with an accident—God forbid. A good Catholic, she crossed herself.

As she dialed, it occurred to her for the first time that language might be a problem. But it wasn't. After she introduced herself, everyone seemed more than happy to speak English. For small blessings she was truly thankful.

None of the three hospitals had a patient listed under the names of Nicholson or Fenimore. Doyle was torn between relief and disappointment. She had another idea. What was the doctor's cousins' name? She had heard it often enough. She racked her brain. It was like a sieve lately. She wished she had Horatio's memory.

She went to the window and looked down. People were strolling by with coats open and heads bare. The day must have grown balmy. What was the doctor's cousin's maiden name? She used it professionally. Mrs. Doyle had heard it often enough. She turned back to the room. *B* . . . She was sure it began with a *B*. She sat on the edge of the bed and leafed through the *B*'s in the phone book. Balik, Bosnik, Borovy . . . *That's it! And she knew his cousin's first name was Anna.* Mrs. Doyle began calling the hospitals once more.

# CHAPTER 50

For the next twenty-four hours, Fenimore kept a close eye on Vlasta. He suffered severe chest pain after the slightest exertion, such as washing his face or brushing his teeth; it was only a small step from such symptoms to a major heart attack. Put very simply, Vlasta's heart was not receiving enough blood. At least one of his arteries was blocked. Fenimore could not make a more specific diagnosis until he had an evaluation. This was what he had been arranging for Vlasta to have done in the States, before he and Anna had disappeared. At that time, Vlasta still had been able to go up a flight of stairs without discomfort. But his condition had worsened during the past few weeks. Thanks to Redik and Ilsa.

The hospital reminded Fenimore of one in which he had interned in the 1970s. Their cardiology was of about the same vintage. He had to tell the doctors, the nurses, even the technicians what to do. Diplomatically, of course. It was a full-time job, with no time off for eating or sleeping.

Jennifer hung around the hospital, supplying Fenimore with coffee and snacks from the cafeteria, and visiting with Anna when she was awake. Unlike her husband, Anna was not desperately ill. Suffering only from exhaustion and mental stress, she would probably be ready to leave the hospital after a few days' rest. As soon as they were settled in the ambulance, Anna demanded to hear about Marie. Fenimore told her she was safe in America.

"America?" She was flabbergasted. She had been told Marie was kidnapped—nothing more. Of course, as soon as they had thought Marie's life was in danger, Anna and Vlasta had revealed their discovery of the hidden staircase and the secret door to the crown jewels. Soon afterwards, Ilsa learned that the crown jewels would be on display at the Coronation Ceremony, making them easily accessible. There was no longer any need for the manuscript that Ilsa had stolen.

Fenimore explained to Anna the necessity of sending Marie out of the country and assured her that she was in good hands. He didn't mention that he had been calling Mrs. Doyle in the States periodically to confirm this, but so far he had been unable to reach her. Shortly afterwards, Anna slipped into a deep sleep, the sleep of utter exhaustion. She slept for twelve hours. By the time she woke, Fenimore was able to give her more positive news about her husband. The medicines were working and he was resting comfortably. There was a possibility that he could fly to the States in a week or two. But Fenimore was still uneasy about Marie. And where could Doyle be?

Once, while paying for coffee in the hospital cafeteria, Jennifer found in the bottom of her purse the sheet of paper that she had confiscated from Redik's basement.

Sharing a rare coffee break with Fenimore, she spread the sheet out on the table and translated, in halting German:

## Manifesto

I, Jan Redik,

do swear to rule the Czech Republic and Prague

—the Jewel in her Crown—

with the same Wise and Beneficent hand as our Great and Good Ruler

Emperor, Charles IV.

Following in his footsteps, I will see that my people never want for

Culture and Education

or

Shoes and Bread.

*Jan Redik*

When she finished, Fenimore made no comment. Either he was too exhausted to comprehend, or he thought it wasn't worthy of his notice.

Jennifer decided it was time to try out her conspiracy theory on him, complete with cell groups and subliminal puppet shows.

"Hmm," Fenimore mused. "Redik might be just crazy enough . . ." And that would explain why there was no reference to freedom or independence in that puppet show.

"Don't you see," Jennifer pointed at the manifesto, "this proves Redik had a plan to take over the Czech Republic. He wanted to turn it into a benevolent dictatorship with himself at the helm, a modern-day Emperor Charles IV!"

"And Ilsa?"

"The *Empress*! Remember, I read you about Charles IV's wife, who could bend a sword with her bare hands? With a little fitness instruction, Ilsa could probably fill that niche very nicely."

Jennifer thought Fenimore was warming to the idea, but his eyelids were drooping. She doubted if he could stay awake much longer.

Taking matters into her own hands, she insisted that he go to her hotel room, which was nearby, and get some sleep. "You can be back in the hospital at a moment's notice," she told him. He finally agreed. Once in her room, he fell onto the bed and slept the sleep of the dead. A few hours later, Jennifer arrived and fell beside him.

They woke in the early evening and felt refreshed. Fenimore called the hospital. His cousins were doing well. Vlasta was resting comfortably and Anna was scheduled for release the next morning. But Ilsa's comment about Marie and the zoo still nagged at him. He shared his concern with Jennifer.

"Why don't you call Dad?" she said. "Maybe he knows something."

He called.

"Nicholson's Bookstore!" a childish voice with a faintly foreign accent sang out.

"Marie?"

"*Ano.* I mean, 'Yes'?"

"Are you okay?"

"Sure."

Fenimore's laugh bordered on the hysterical.

"You want to buy a book, Uncle Andrew?" Marie chirped.

"No—no, thanks." Choking back his laughter, he told Marie that her parents were okay, too, and she would see them soon. When he hung up, Jennifer looked bewildered.

"Everything's okay," he said, although he still had not located his elusive nurse, cum baby-sitter. But she was probably doing errands while Marie was at the bookstore, he decided. "What now?" He searched Jennifer's face.

"Let's go out on the town," she suggested.

"You mean it?"

"Sure. We'll get you that wonderful Czech dinner you've been longing for."

His eyes lit up. "Honest?"

"Absolutely. But first let's take a walk along the river, stop at a wine bar. . . . I love the city at twilight."

Fenimore stared at her.

"What's wrong?"

"You've forgiven me?"

"For what?"

"Ilsa."

"Oh, that." She shrugged. "You were seduced. It happens."

"Was not."

"Was."

"Not."

"Was."

He came over to the bed and put his arms around her. "Wasn't," he murmured in her ear.

She drew back. "Do you prefer big women?"

Fenimore scratched his head. "Well, I've always wondered. . . ."

Jennifer began beating his chest with her fists.

Grabbing her hands, he silenced her.

# CHAPTER 51

On her second call, Mrs. Doyle hit pay dirt. The hospital where Fenimore's cousins were registered as patients was just a tram-ride away from her hotel. She hopped on a tram and for the first time relaxed and looked at the old city. "Old" was the feeling that pervaded her. Everywhere she looked were buildings, pitted and tarnished with age—like old silver. And, like old silver, they glowed with the luster, warmth, and dignity acquired by age. They absorbed their modern additions, such as a neon sign here or a bright awning there, with the ease of an old dowager donning a new hat or carrying a new purse. Even the occasional graffiti failed to disfigure them, blending with their ancient scars and stains. They had withstood the test of time. Next to them, Independence Hall, with its red bricks and white trim, seemed like a young upstart.

In the hospital lobby, Mrs. Doyle stopped at the front desk for a visitor's card and took the elevator to Anna's room, on the third floor. They would not let her see Vlasta who was in the ICU, because she wasn't a relative. (Some things are the same the world over.)

Anna's door was ajar. She tapped lightly and went in. The woman was dozing, but opened her eyes when Mrs. Doyle spoke. "Forgive me, I'm looking for Dr. Fenimore," she said. "He's a friend of mine."

She didn't want to upset the woman with too many lengthy explanations.

"I'm sorry. He left about . . ." She frowned. "You lose track of time in here. . . . About two hours ago. Poor man. He was exhausted from looking after my husband and me."

"Was there a woman with him?"

"Oh, yes. A lovely young woman. Jennifer."

Mrs. Doyle's legs felt wobbly. She sat down on the nearest chair. She hadn't realized how great her fears had been until they were eliminated.

"Yes," Anna said, "please sit down. You look worn-out."

With her practiced nurse's eye, Mrs. Doyle recognized that Anna was not seriously ill. Mrs. Doyle revealed her identity, and told Anna that she had been with her daughter just hours ago.

Anna's eyes filled with tears as Mrs. Doyle recounted some of Marie's recent antics in Philadelphia. But when she described Marie taking her teddy bear to the zoo, her mother laughed out loud. "That bear!" she said. "She takes him everywhere."

"She must inherit that from the doctor. He still keeps his bear on the end of his bed."

"No!"

Seeing that Anna was relaxed, Mrs. Doyle ventured to ask about her recent experience.

Slowly, Anna recounted the story of their kidnapping, imprisonment, and rescue.

"Mercy!" The word was inadequate to sum up Mrs. Doyle's feelings. After a moment, she asked where the doctor and Jennifer were now.

Anna gave her the name and address of Jennifer's hotel.

The danger past, Mrs. Doyle felt no urgency to rush there. She lingered to tell Anna more about her child, a subject a mother never grows tired of.

When she finally left the hospital, Mrs. Doyle was surprised to find it had grown dark. Unfamiliar with the crime-rate in Prague, she decided to splurge and take a cab to Jennifer's hotel. As the cab drew up to the hotel entrance, she spied the doctor and Jennifer coming out. Walking hand in hand they looked so happy, she couldn't bear to disturb them. Incurable romantic that she was, she decided to return to her own hotel and wait until morning to make her presence known. She was about to give the driver her address, when she noticed two figures step from the shadows of a doorway and follow her friends. She quickly paid the driver and got out of the cab.

# CHAPTER 52

It was after nine when they left the hotel room. So much for twilight. But evening in Prague wasn't so bad. For the first time since he arrived, Fenimore felt relaxed and happy. He was completely unaware of the two scruffy, tattooed youths a few yards behind them, and of course, of Mrs. Doyle. He was aware only of the pressure of Jennifer's hand. He returned it. "Where to?" he asked.

"No plan," she said dreamily. "Let's just wander."

And so they did, through the crooked gaslit streets, over the ancient cobblestones. Turning right, then left, and left again, completely unaware of the trouble they were causing the three people hot on their heels behind them.

"This looks nice." Jennifer paused at an open doorway, from which melodious music wafted. Music was everywhere in Prague, Fenimore noticed. "The Queen of Music,' Mozart called the city," he told Jennifer. Inside were tables, each bearing a vase of fresh flowers and a flickering candle. They went in. They didn't talk much, content to sip their wine, stare at the candle flame and, now and then, at each other. Fenimore recognized the music in the background—a piano concerto by Mozart. He roused himself to say, "Mozart was a favorite son of Praguers. It was here that *Don Gio-*

*vanni* was first performed and acclaimed. Not Vienna."

"To Don Giovanni!" Jennifer raised her glass. "Wait a minute." She lowered her glass. "Wasn't he that unscrupulous Casanova?"

"Umm." Fenimore had the grace to blush.

After two glasses of wine, Fenimore said, "I'm hungry."

"I read about a restaurant in my guidebook," she said. "It's across the Charles Bridge and known for its traditional Czech dinners."

Visions of succulent schnitzel, dumplings, and *palačinky* rose before him as he helped Jennifer on with her coat. Taking her arm he guided her out to the street and looked up and down. Which way was the Charles Bridge? he wondered. They had made so many turns he had lost his bearings. It took them a while to find the bridge, and their followers cursed them roundly. Even Mrs. Doyle resorted to a few swear words. "Where the hell are they going?" she muttered. "These damned cobblestones are killing my feet!" She blamed this verbal lapse on her recent close association with Horatio. To atone, she said a few Hail Marys.

The bridge was less crowded now. The vendors had left and the few strollers were taking their time, pausing to gaze at the river in the moonlight. The statues of heroes and saints cast shadows across their path.

They paused too, to look at the river.

"Was your mother ever homesick?" Jennifer asked, unexpectedly.

He remembered that night long ago, when he had observed his mother after the opera. "Yes," he said, "I'm afraid she was."

"It would be hard to leave a place like this—especially if it was your home."

"True. But when your home is desecrated and under the rule of a ruthless foreign power, it makes it easier."

"I suppose. . . ."

Fenimore did not want to be reminded of his mother just now. She would not have approved of his conduct since he had arrived in Prague. He blushed to think what she would have had to say about it. "But I did save the crown!" he reminded his mother's reproving ghost.

To reach the restaurant, they had to go down some steps and take a path that wound through the trees along the river. The air was full of the smell of growing things and the moon danced through the branches, lighting their way. At one point, Jennifer made Fenimore climb over some old, creosoted logs and onto a wharf, to get a better view of the Charles Bridge from the river. The statues were silhouetted in the soft glow of the lamps and a fine mist was rising from the water. Fenimore chose this moment to turn her face toward his and. . . . fall into the river.

Jennifer quickly followed.

But they didn't fall; they were pushed. And when they came spluttering to the surface, the pushers were poised on the wharf, oars raised, ready to whack them over their heads—which they did.

That was the last Jennifer and Fenimore remembered.

Their assailants melted into the trees. The riverbank was empty except for one lone jogger. Breathing hard, the overweight, middle-aged woman thumped down the path toward the river.

Mrs. Doyle put her handbag down on the bank and removed her shoes. She stared intently at the water. First Fenimore, then Jennifer bobbed to the surface. Their eyes were closed and they disappeared immediately. *One more chance,* she told herself, and jumped into the river. After the first shock of cold water, she pulled one of the nearby logs in after her. When Fenimore popped up this time, she yelled, "Doctor!" and shoved the log under him. His eyelids fluttered open and he grabbed it. Treading water, Mrs. Doyle waited for Jennifer. When she surfaced, the nurse yelled her name and shoved another log under her. Shaking the water out of her eyes, Jennifer grabbed it. Mrs. Doyle, teeth chattering, maneuvered herself behind her two friends. Placing one hand on each of their bottoms, she kicked furiously, pushing them toward shore. They lay like two miniature whales, flopping and gasping, while Mrs. Doyle crawled out and joined them. If it hadn't been for her karate training, she never could have done this.

She didn't know how long they lay there, but when she opened her eyes, the lights on the bridge were no longer glowing, there was a streak of pink in the sky, and she was numb with cold. She glanced at her companions. Neither was stirring. She forced herself to her feet and began to rouse them.

When Fenimore opened his eyes and saw Mrs. Doyle bending over him, he felt like Noah when he first saw the dove with the olive branch, or Balboa when he first glimpsed the Pacific, or Lindbergh when he first sighted Paris.

"How did *you* get here?" he asked, drinking her in.

"Angel's wings."

"I believe it," he said reverently.

# CHAPTER 53

Back at the hotel, Fenimore showered, shaved, dressed, and realized that his problems were far from over. How could he leave his cousins in Prague, with their enemies still at large? It would be several weeks before Vlasta would be strong enough to come to the States for his evaluation. Fenimore's recent experience with the police had not increased his confidence in them. Whom could he turn to for help?

He glanced at the newspaper Jennifer had handed him along with a cup of steaming coffee from the lobby. The *Prague Times*. The only English-Czech paper, it was distributed to hotel lobbies free, primarily for the benefit of American tourists. There, on the front page, was a picture of the one person he could trust. The one person in Prague he knew was incorruptible. But he had no way to gain his ear. He had no contacts, no influence, no clout. Fenimore could hardly walk into the president's office at Prague Castle and say: "Hi! I'm an American, but my mother was Czech, and I've read all your plays. How 'bout helping me with this problem . . . ?"

He shook his head and turned the page. A headline leapt out at him:

Three photos accompanied the article: Ema, pretty, in a dewy, unformed way; Redik, resembling one of the lesser Roman emperors; and Ilsa—looking like a rose in full bloom—the way she had looked that first day in the coffeehouse.

According to the story, Ilsa had discovered Ema and Redik in his dressing room, in a compromising position, and stabbed them to death.

Fenimore felt dizzy. He heard Ema's shrill voice defending the puppets. He saw Redik's mad dance on the tower. He felt the tingle of Ilsa's touch. . . .

Charles IV's curse, it seems, was still intact. And Fenimore was not entirely glad.

He stared at the three photos again.

When Jennifer emerged from the shower, wrapped in a towel, he showed her the article. She sat on the edge of the bed, biting her lip. "Why do I feel so bad?"

Fenimore didn't answer.

"For her, I guess." Jennifer indicated Ema's picture. "And I never even met her."

"I met her," he said slowly, refolding the paper. "Redik's marionettes have lost a friend."

Anna was to be released that morning. When Fenimore arrived at the hospital, he went to check Vlasta first. His condition was steadily improving. Fenimore felt confident he could safely leave his cousin and return to the States. But it would be several weeks before Vlasta could travel by plane and come to Philadelphia for his cardiac evaluation. Anna, of course, would stay with her husband in Prague. But what about Marie? Fenimore would like to keep her in Philadelphia until her parents arrived. But, by then, school would be in session. . . .

These thoughts flitted through his mind, on one level, as he made his way along the corridor to Anna's room. On another, deeper level,

190

lay the news of Ilsa—like a coiled snake. He had known double-murderers before, but not quite in the same way. He was still numb from the shock. When the numbness wore off and the snake un-coiled, he wasn't sure what his reaction would be. With effort, he concentrated on his family problems.

When Fenimore entered Anna's room, she was sitting on the bed, fully dressed, speaking animatedly in Czech on the phone. Mrs. Doyle was sitting nearby, leafing through a magazine. She looked up, pointed to the phone, and mouthed, *Marie.*

Fenimore smiled. This was not the time to tell her about the murders.

After consulting with Anna, it was decided that Marie should stay in Philadelphia until her parents arrived. Anna would have to tolerate this further separation from her child, and Marie could make up what she had missed at school. She was very clever, and third grade was not that difficult, after all.

Fenimore accompanied Anna home in a cab. During the ride, he showed her the newspaper article. It didn't have the impact Fenimore had expected. After her recent experiences, Anna was impervious to shock. The human psyche can absorb only so much; Anna's had reached the saturation point. Scanning the article, she returned the paper to Fenimore with a mere shake of the head.

When Anna entered her apartment, she walked from room to room taking everything in; touching a book here, a lamp there—to make sure they were real. "I thought I would never be here again," she explained. "Yet, here I am . . . thanks to you and Jennifer."

Fenimore quietly went about collecting his things. He had decided to spend the rest of his stay with Jennifer, at her hotel, and leave his cousin to enjoy her homecoming in peace. He had told her that he had retrieved the manuscript. And there it sat, snugly in the bookcase, where he had stowed it. Before he left, Fenimore told Anna that he had paid the April rent.

"What?" She was dismayed. "I already paid for April. We always pay a month in advance." She shook her head in disgust as she wrote him a check. "That horrible man. He sneaks around here, eaves-dropping. And I think he runs some illegal business from the basement. Black market, smuggling, or—"

"Marie is afraid of him," Fenimore interrupted.

"She is?"

"I think he may have hurt her once."

"No!" Her ability to react was returning.

Fenimore described Marie's strange behavior on the day they were to leave for the airport.

Anna's eyes narrowed and her fists clenched. "I'll take care of him," she said.

And Fenimore knew she would.

"By the way," he said in parting, "be sure to order some pizza now and then. Milo is a good friend."

Anna looked after his retreating back with a bewildered expression.

Fenimore returned to the hotel to find Jennifer packing.

"I've made our plane reservations," she said. "Mrs. Doyle's, too. Our flight leaves tomorrow morning at eleven-thirty."

He nodded, preoccupied.

"Is that too soon?" She was afraid she had been officious.

"What?"

"Would you rather leave later?"

"No." He wandered over to the window and looked out. "There's that picture of Kafka's house that I have to take for Larry. . . ."

"We can go this afternoon."

"You know"—he turned back to the room—"Redik was mad! Did he really believe he could conquer the Czech Republic—and specifically Prague—through subliminal propaganda via puppets?"

"Don't forget the crown. He thought it had mystical powers."

"In a psychology course I took at college, we watched a movie that glorified the German Youth Movement," Fenimore said. "It had been made during the Hitler era. The teacher told us he had to break it up into four segments, with ten-minute intermissions, otherwise we might all be converted. We laughed, scornfully, of course. But, do you know—even *with* the intermissions—we all came out of that film marching and singing and wanting to join up?"

"You're kidding."

"I kid you not. Little Fritz was so cute, and the music was so strong. . . . Never underestimate the power of the media, whether film, radio, TV—or puppets. Goebbels knew this. He once said that Americans didn't need a propaganda ministry, they had Hollywood."

"*Casablanca* is a good example," Jennifer agreed. "When they sing 'La Marseillaise,' I'd do anything for them."

"The thing I don't understand is why Ilsa bought into it. She seemed like an intelligent—"

"Love."

He looked at her sharply.

"Why do you think I hang around with you?" she said.

"You think *I'm* crazy?"

"Well, every now and then . . ."

After a long silence, he said, "I wonder what Ilsa would have been like, if she had achieved her dream."

Jennifer paused in her packing. "And what was that?"

"To be an actress," he said.

"She *was* an actress," Jennifer said tersely. "And a very good one."

He couldn't deny that.

"And her last act was worthy of a Verdi opera!"

After a while, Jennifer forced herself to ask, "Do you want to see her before we leave?"

"Hell, no." He headed for the door. "Let's go take that picture."

As they made their way to Golden Lane, Jennifer asked, "Where is our lifeguard today?"

"On a bus tour of Prague. I thought she should see something of the city before she left. You know what she said? 'I'll go anywhere as long as it's not on foot.' Apparently cobblestones and Doyle's feet are incompatible."

"She does better on sea than land. Where did she learn those lifesaving techniques?"

"She was a Navy nurse . . . and keeps fit with karate."

"There it is." Jennifer stopped in front of a stucco cottage with a crooked chimney and reached into her purse. She handed Fenimore the cheap little camera she had picked up at the airport.

Fenimore took two pictures of Kafka's house.

Jennifer scanned the guidebook. "Kafka lived in about a dozen places in Prague. Should we take them all?"

"One's enough for Larry," Fenimore said emphatically. He took a picture of Jennifer leaning over the wall, gazing at the city. Then *she* took one of Fenimore leaning over the wall, gazing at the city.

A woman was about to walk between them, but paused so she wouldn't spoil their picture. Then she said, "Would you like me to take one of you together?"

They smiled self-consciously, and Fenimore handed her the camera.

*Click.*

"Thanks so much."

"Yes, thanks."

"No problem." She walked on.

They took the steep, cobblestone path back to the city.

# The Feast

"... he who does not mind his belly, will hardly mind
anything else."
Samuel Johnson in *Boswell's Life of Johnson*

# EPILOGUE

They were all gathered at Fenimore's dining-room table. Vlasta was seated at one end, Anna at the other. Marie, Jiri, Horatio, Mrs. Doyle, Jennifer, Mr. Nicholson, and Detective Rafferty completed the party. The latter could hardly be left out when he had played such an important role in the zoo episode. Fenimore had been filled in on that when he returned and he was extremely grateful to Horatio and Rafferty for their rescue of Marie. (Horatio's reward had come in the form of a state-of-the-art yo-yo.) And Fenimore had been properly chagrined when he realized that he had played a part in the attempted kidnapping. If he had been more astute and less taken with Ilsa, he might have noticed her reading Jennifer's email address over his shoulder at the cyber café and prevented her from setting up the whole scheme.

Anna had prepared the dinner—a traditional Czech feast with all the trimmings. Fenimore had introduced her to the Reading Terminal Market, where she had spent a wonderful day roaming among the stalls, exchanging pleasantries in German with the Pennsylvania Dutch farmers and selecting all the ingredients. The celebration was for Vlasta. His "Welcome Home" party, or his coming-out party—from the hospital, where he had received his new stent—the clever device by which his artery would be kept open, allowing blood to flow freely to his heart.

*How ironic,* thought Fenimore, *that I had to wait until I got back to Philadelphia to have a bona fide Czech dinner.* He looked around the table at his friends and relatives. *Everyone I care about is either at this table—or under it.* (Sal was nibbling at his shoelaces.) He reached down and gave her a piece of schnitzel. "Did you know," he interrupted the general conversation, "that President Masaryk came to Philadelphia in 1918 and read *your* Declaration of Independence at *our* Independence Hall?" They were all speaking English now.

"What did you say, Andrew?" Anna asked.

He repeated what he had said more slowly, then added, "And tomorrow I will take you all to see the Liberty Bell."

"Jiri, too?" asked Marie.

"Jiri, too."

"I've seen it," Rafferty protested, "a million times." His office was located in the Police Administration Building only a few blocks from Independence Hall.

"Well, you're excused," Fenimore said, "although I don't think it would hurt you to see it again."

Rafferty snorted.

"Lovely." Anna nodded, agreeable to the idea. Then she pointed her camera at Fenimore and said, "Smile."

Fenimore looked straight into the lens and smiled (forgetting, for the moment, about his ears).

Conversation dwindled as they concentrated on their palačinky filled with prune butter, topped with melted butter, confectioner's sugar, and sour cream. (Except for the guest of honor, of course. Poor Vlasta was on a low-cholesterol diet and had to make do with stewed apricots.)